DAY ONE
TALES OF THE SCOUR
BOOK 1

BLAZE WARD

Day One
Tales From the Scour: 1
Blaze Ward
Copyright © 2025 Blaze Ward
All rights reserved
Published by Knotted Road Press
www.KnottedRoadPress.com

ISBN: 978-1-64470-467-7
Cover Art:ID 318092512 © Sabelskaya | Dreamstime.com
ID 250010375 © 1971yes | Dreamstime.com

Cover and interior design copyright © 2025 Knotted Road Press

Reviews
It's true. Reviews help. Even a short one, such as, "Loved it!" So please consider reviewing this book (and all of the ones you've read) on your favorite retailer site.

Never miss a release!
If you'd like to be notified of new releases, sign up for my newsletter.

http://www.blazeward.com/newsletter/

Buy More!
Did you know that you can buy directly from the Knotted Road Press website?

https://www.knottedroadpress.com/shop/

ALSO BY BLAZE WARD

The Science Officer Series

Start with: The Science Officer

The Jessica Keller Chronicles

Start with: Auberon

CS-405 (Command Centurion Kosnett, part of Jessica)

Start with: Queen Anne's Revenge

First Centurion Kosnett (sequel to Jessica)

Start with: Encounter at Vilahana

Additional Alexandria Station Stories

Alexandria Station Collection

Handsome Rob (Alexandria Station Universe)

Start with: Can't Shoot Straight Gang

=====================

Corsac Fox

Start with: Flight of the Corsac Fox

Operation Marrakesh

Start with: Trial by Leviathan

Captain Daring

Start with: Revoked

The Hunter Bureau

Start with: Mirrors

Fairchild

Start with: Fairchild

Last Stand

Start with: Lost Dreams

The Lazarus Alliance

Start with: Escape

Shadow of the Dominion

Start with: Longshot Hypothesis

Star Dragon

Start with: Birth of the Star Dragon

Kincaide's War

Start with: The Eden Package

Star Tribes

Start with: Winterstar

Blaze also writes Action-Adventure Here

It wasn't the way he would have liked it, but Duff didn't really figure he had a lot of options today.

He hadn't originally been scheduled to report to his new job for another couple of days, but then one of the kids had called in sick this morning, and the dispatcher had pulled up his name as first alternate. So here he was.

All of his worldly goods were stuff in the oversized gear bag slung across his back, like he was going out in the desert sun again today. Instead, for at least a little while, he was safe underground from the Scour, those terrible storms that had wrecked civilization centuries ago and were intent on pulling everything back down as soon any time the folks of the Nine Cities dared rebuild. Hell, he still had three spare barrels as well as his rifle stuck in there, just because he hadn't had time to make arrangements to store everything with the call coming so early this morning.

The dim tunnels were cool and almost abandoned as he walked. Undercity never saw the sun, but the SkyFolk, up in their protected domes, lived an old-fashioned lifestyle, rising and setting with the sun overhead. The Scour winds couldn't penetrate the domes with their electrical charges. All they could do was sling grit against it. Eventually, a panel would fog and someone would go up on a ladder and a rope and replace it.

Still a much safer job on the worst day that being a lineman out in the desert.

Except Duff wasn't a lineman anymore. Wouldn't be, in spite of the union rules that had protected him that much. Even they had limits

He sighed as he found the door to the rail yard. Entering, it was like a vast, underground cathedral from some fairly tale, seemingly stretched out forever, low and wide, lit inadequately by the lamps overhead.

Duff wasn't sure whether to be elated or disappointed with the new job. He could see the enormous cowcatcher on the front of the train *City of Angels* in the distance, that massive engine, four stories tall, forged in a black, rigid polymer that made it look almost like a beast from the pit.

The Scour would induce a current in any bar or sheet of ferrous metal that it could, so they insulated the machines as much as possible. And anything that could conduct electricity when the lightning hit. The Undercity had wells drilled deep to draw petroleum up from the inky depths, where it could be turned into all manner of magical things, since most metals weren't safe.

Maybe not as good as steel, but it also wouldn't kill you if a storm hit while you were out in the open.

Duff wasn't assigned to *City of Angels*. Didn't even really know the next time that beast was scheduled to depart. When he was a still a lineman, like yesterday, his job had been fixing rail beds and the underground telephone lines that linked the nine cities together in a web of civilization.

Or whatever it was.

He sure as hell didn't know what a *Fireman* did on a train, but Duff figured it couldn't be that hard to learn, since that was the job the youngest kids got when they first came aboard. At thirty-eight, he wasn't a snot-nosed punk anymore. Well, not snot-nosed, anyway.

Punk might be a whole different story.

He reached into an inside pocket of his desert longcoat and pulled out the telegram. Compared where he was standing to where it said to go. Checked the big, luminescent clock on the wall with numbers as tall as he was.

Early still, and on track.

He turned to his right and made his way across the stone floor, eyes and ears tracking everything, just like he was on the surface and something terrible might be coming for him. Train engines made a lot of noise, but he knew that sometimes a hostler would get up a head of steam then detach some cars, letting them run down a track with the switchers rerouting it, until it bounced noisily into another train and attached itself for the next run.

Down in one corner he found his goal. *Postmaster Seventeen*. The Mail Train.

It was one of the small ones. Only ran on one pair of side-by-side tracks, on a standard gauge just under a meter and a half wide. The big beasts, trains like *City of Angels*, treated that whole pair as a side and had an eight-meter gap to the other side pair, spanning the width like a bridge that went on forever and ever.

A rolling city. Or maybe a fortress, since you occasionally

ran into all sorts of weird creatures out in the desert, to say nothing of the storms.

Postmaster Seventeen was tiny by comparison. A small engine up front, wrapped all around in those insulating plastic plates that would protect some of the metal underneath. The box behind that, completely insulated by a Faraday cage, where the engineer and his kid rode. Small personnel car for the crew attached to the engine as a team. Three cars behind that, long rolling boxes filled with the mail, from postcards all the way up to packages the size of two coffins stacked. Anything larger rode on the big girls, like *City of Angels.*

Duff walked up to the side of the engine and looked at his new job. The side door was just slightly ajar, with a warm, yellow-tinged light spilling out. It was almost like the engineer had an actual fire going inside, rather than a wall of batteries and all the solar panels on the roof.

Like the ancient legends, when a fireman was the guy who shoveled coal into the boiler.

Duff checked his bag and set one heavy boot onto the bottom rung of the ladder, pulling himself up with his left hand. It had been so sudden that he hadn't even been issued a new uniform, so he was reporting for work this morning in his desert gear, like he had for the last twenty-some years.

And he didn't trust a locker somewhere while he was gone, so that meant everything came with him. Field bag. Heavy, lace-up boots. Desert pants with the semi-rigid armor plates you might need if a snake or lizard popped out from some-where and tried to bite you.

Over his only nice shirt, the white one, he had that the old, battered armorvest, the one you wore for protecting ribs in case you fell off a ledge. It had belonged to his dad, back when ol' Thorstein was a still Skipboss.

Hell, he'd even worn his brown longcoat this morning, just because. The summer hat was in his bag.

The only thing missing was the revolver on his hip and the rifle on his shoulder, both broken down for storage in the bag, because he doubted that the engineer in charge would appreciate him showing up armed on his first day as junior-most peon on the rails.

Duff climbed up onto the little platform and pulled the hatch out, slipping quietly in.

He knew Acheson Innes by reputation, but only vaguely in person. It was a small world underground, but not that small. Even the various transportation unions had several thousand members.

But *Postmaster Seventeen* wasn't that bad, at least as far as the stories went. Duff figured he could have drawn much worse on his first run.

The old man was seated at his controls, apparently going over a checklist on a transparent clipboard. Tall and rangy, but much thinner than a lineman like Duff. Not as tan, but his time outside the city would generally be in the air-conditioned cab of a train like this, driving the mail back and forth.

Innes looked up and studied him for a long moment. The light in here was a little dim. That moment at dawn, just before the blazing hot sun exploded above the horizon and started baking everything in another day of dry heat.

"When I saw the roster this morning, I assumed you had a nephew or something," Innes said in a slow, comfortable drawl with almost no emotion behind it. "*Torcuil Dubhthaigh.* Couldn't be *Duff*, could it?"

Duff shrugged and slipped the bag off his back, sliding it into a quiet corner away from controls and seats, at least until he was told where to stow it.

"Wasn't supposed to start the new job until Wednesday," he answered, trying not to sound evasive with his new boss. "Someone moved me up in the rotation. Hopefully that means my seniority gets bumped two days, as well."

Innes rose now with the faintest grin on his clean-shaved mouth. He was a little taller than Duff, but again, built like a skeleton. He held out a hand and Duff took it.

"So how is it I end up with Duff as my fireman, anyway, son?" the man asked.

He could get away with that kind of language. Acheson Innes had something like two decades on him. Had to be at least in his late fifties now.

Duff considered his response. He hadn't planned too much of this conversation ahead of time, not knowing what the old man would be like as a person.

"Union rules," he said carefully, drawing a bit of surprise from Innes's face.

Duff took that as a good sign and continued.

"If they wanted to fire me for insubordination, then that would have triggered a full grievance process," he said. "A whole lot of ugliness would have come out under oath, if they tried something that stupid with me."

"I see," the man replied carefully, stepping back to study him closer in the confines of the cabin. "So they transferred you to the rail division and made you a fireman?"

"Contract says I keep my pension at whatever my highest year of income was," Duff shrugged. "Been a Senior Lineman for five years now. Even if I spend the next three years as a fireman, I'll have my twenty-five at a nice lifestyle for whatever I do with the rest of my life. It was a bad compromise, but nobody got all the short end all to themselves."

"And you're okay being the scut on everything, Duff?" he asked.

Duff shrugged. He'd been out on the desert floor for a week or more at a time, doing hard labor and watching for nasty things trying to sneak up on him. There was nothing that could happen on a train engine that would be nearly as hard or fretful. And he seriously doubted the union bosses would ever put him on a city train like *Angels*, where he might run into the beautiful people and spoil their days just by existing.

Pretty boys and girls got those gigs, not desert mutts like him.

"I'm stubborn enough to handle this for three year, Innes," Duff replied. "Hell, I could stand on my head for three years to get a good pension. If that means cleaning bathrooms and running errands, I've done worse."

"All right," the old man said, turning. "Bring your bag and I'll show you were you stow it, then we'll get you to work. Pretty sure the bathroom is clean enough, at least for now."

That last was said glancing back with a grin on his face, so Duff figured the old man was just going to have a little fun with him, rather than some of the nasty hazing a senior man like this Engineer might do to a young fireman just getting started in life.

They passed out of the cab and into the second car of the train. Hallway down the center, with doors on both sides. Innes opened the one on the right and stepped past.

Duff entered into a closet just long enough for him to lay down on one of the two bunk beds, but tall enough that he had space to sit up. He reached under the bottom bunk and pulled out the hardbox he saw, opening it enough to drop his stuff in and closing it up. Didn't bother locking it for now, since he'd need to sort everything out later, once they were in motion.

He turned and found Innes further back in the hallway, where the walls ended and opened up to a room the full width of the car.

"Kitchen and coffee are here," he said, pointing. "Breakfast nook over there. Part of your job is supposed to be learning how to cook, but I'm going to assume you're already past that, so we'll figure out a meal schedule once you inventory the refrigerator and pantry. Questions?"

"What's your favorite meal of the day?" Duff asked.

"Usually supper," Innes smiled. "Run like this down to Jacumba, we'll see *Postmaster Four* headed north about an hour before sunset, this time of year. I like to have some coffee around then, before we slow down to a crawl when it gets too dark, so that we can pick up early at false dawn and maybe make it to the end of the line about sunrise."

Duff nodded. He could see three big meals, or maybe one big one in the afternoon and a rolling series of snacks as the day progressed, plus staying up all night to keep Innes company and awake. According to the schedule they'd sleep in Jacumba as the crews detached cargo, spun them around on the big wheel, and then got everything ready for a run north late in the day.

It was a thankless job, but you had to keep the wheels of commerce rolling, even if a Scour threatened to destroy anything people built. At least the train was heavy enough and streamlined not to be at risk if something like those killer winds came down on them.

"Let's tour the rest and then you can get settled in," Innes said. "We're about an hour or so from them throwing open the gates and sending us on our way."

Duff followed the tall man to the rear, noting everything and confirming the warning signs marked on various panels and boxes. The union might be run by assholes, but they didn't skimp on the little things.

And how bad could it be to be a fireman for a few years until he could retire?

CHAPTER 2

Duff had changed clothes. Some. Found a spare pair of pants someone had left behind, tucked into the other box. Not the one where his gear was stashed. The pants were too big around the waist but long enough, and came with suspenders that would hold them up for a few days.

And it wasn't like he didn't know how to take in a pair of pants, once Acheson said he didn't care what happened to them. Armorvest and longcoat went into the small closet tucked in at the end of his cabin. That left him in the white shirt and wrong pants, but Innes just laughed the first time Duff walked into the cabin bringing the man coffee.

There wasn't anything he could do about his boots, except practice walking quieter on the heavy black plates that made up the deck around here. He was used to sand and stone, and the toe caps would stop most things, all the way up to bullets fired from a ways off. Saved his ass a few times with sudden gila monsters.

Coffeemaker in the kitchen was union standard. Interestingly, identical to the one Duff had in his mess kit, where it was intended for one man to be able to make himself a big mug, rather than doing enough for a team.

Made sense though, when he thought about it. The crew of a Postmaster train was usually two or maybe three people at most, so you weren't generally needing to make big meals either.

Maybe riding a train wasn't going to be all that different from being out working lines. Sure, you had a foreman over thirty-five or forty people, but usually things got broken down into eight or maybe a dozen under a Skipboss if you had a big job, each team heading off to do different things.

Most of the time Duff had ended up off on some stretch along with a couple of other linemen and maybe a gandy dancer, if they had a kid needed training. Usually those were back with the foreman or a skipboss, but Jack had always liked the way Duff trained them.

"So now what?" Duff asked as he handed a chuckling Acheson a mug, keeping the other one for himself.

"Just waiting for that light there to change to green," he pointed out the front window as he took a sip. "We've got most of our cargo already loaded, but I got a note from Yard Foreman that they were adding a fourth car at the last minute. Some super-secret cargo needs to head down to the coast."

"What do I do?" Duff asked.

"You sit in that seat for now," Acheson gestured. "Normally, the fireman is too green to do anything useful, but they sent me someone with a little more seasoning this time. This is still pushing the margins though."

Duff did as he was bid. Acheson was handling this situation better than Duff had expected. Maybe the man didn't care that Duff had a reputation for stubbornness, but that was usually the result of digging in his heels when someone tried to cut corners.

Safety never came before profit. Not even union bosses and owners were going to get him to move on that.

Of course, that was why he was sitting in the left-hand seat of an engine today, instead of being out in the sun digging up lines usually damaged by ground critters looking for a new den.

He watched as Acheson finally moved the big, black snake forward, switchers waving at them as they approached and passed. Eventually, the train ended up close to the big gate that kept out the winds and storms, as well as the Scour.

Duff watched and learned, memorizing the signals flowing back and forth. They used radio waves underground, where it was safe, so Acheson could talk to a dispatcher over in a tower.

Nothing like that ever really worked out on the surface, but that was just one of the reasons folks had dug into the sides of mountains to escape the storms in the old days.

Or they'd already been there and nobody else had survived. After this long, nobody could separate fact from legend, even when you got lucky and found some old ruins that hadn't already been picked clean by scavengers.

Folks didn't live all that long on the surface either. Too much radiation left over in some places, from when the gods had decided to destroy civilization and let loose destruction. The kind that had created the Scour. Duff had read old books talking about paradise on earth, where water fell softly from the sky and was clean enough to drink without filters and boiling.

Legendary shit like that.

"Ready?" Acheson asked sidelong, breaking a silence so deep Duff wasn't too sure the old man had been awake.

Duff nodded, unsure what was coming.

"Clench your teeth and grab on to the arm rails," Acheson said simply.

Duff did. About a second later, that fourth car slammed into the back of the train hard enough that he might have bitten his tongue off if it had caught him looking the wrong way.

The whole cab had jounced all over the place, and not just him, but Acheson Innes hadn't flinched. Hadn't even blinked.

Like he did this every day. Maybe he did. Duff was still just a fireman on his first day.

"*Postmaster Seventeen*, we show green on all boards," the dispatcher's voice came over the radio. "Please confirm."

Acheson did some things that Duff didn't follow, but mostly it was looking at a variety of gauges in front of him. Duff had an identical set, but hadn't been told what any of them were, and wasn't about to guess.

Fireman. First day. Try not to break anything, kid.

"*Postmaster Seventeen*, I confirm green," Acheson said a moment later. "Ready for the main doors."

Somebody did something, because Duff caught the first hint of light as the big barn doors started to slide sideways back into the rock facing, revealing the valley below and Manah Lake, where the city of Levin drew a lot of its water.

Stuff was mostly clean. Better than the ruined cityscapes further south, where the wars had been fiercest and the water might come up brown on a bad day. Or worse, just kill you if you drank any without running it through the tester first.

He still didn't know how they survived down at Jacumba, other than the bay was close enough to run water up pipelines and into tanks. And the hurricanes were usually broken up enough not to do more than drop acidic rain by the time they got that far inland.

The morning sun filled the cathedral with a different light. Rich and warm. Life-bringing, since it was still early enough that the temperatures would be below thirty-five degrees for a while yet.

Was only supposed to get up to thirty-eight today, practically paradise. And he'd be riding in an air-conditioned cab at around twenty-five degrees, instead of on a flatbed being pushed out to wherever the systems detected a line break. Or headed out to where some earthquake on Andreas had shifted bars around enough to potentially damage the rolling stock.

Fellow could get to liking life like this.

CHAPTER 3

In the darkness of his little nook, Matthias reached into the pocket of his vest and pulled out his watch, pressing the button to illuminate the numbers.

Right on time.

Postmaster Seventeen had shifted forward from the original spot where a forklift had loaded up the first three cars with cargo, and was patiently waiting close to the front doors, while a hostler and his team sent the last car careening across the yard at a fast walk.

It helped that the ground in this rail yard was flat enough to hold a marble in place.

Matthias watched the car slow down incrementally, to the point that it would just kiss the back of the train and connect itself. Truly, there was an art to slinging that many tons of material around.

He glanced back at the shadows behind him, counting once again that the other four members of the gang were present. He had planned this robbery too closely to have something go wrong this late. Scrubbing would cost him a signifi-cant amount of planning and possibly his retirement to a nice city far away where nobody from Levin would ever be able to touch him,

Matthias looked forward to living like a king. He smiled at his two queens now, Lefty and Red. Lefty had a carnivorous look on her face, but that was just the possibility of violence soon. Red was almost her exact opposite in all things, quiet and careful. But you needed those sorts of things if you were going to crack safes and security systems.

Lefty was just a killer, with a revolver on each side of those lovely hips.

Beyond the two women, Lonagan and Pedro lurked. Neither brought any brains to the outfit, but Lonagan was stronger than almost any man Matthias had ever met, with a pain threshold simply unbelievable. Pedro was a strong back, carrying all of Red's heavy tools that she would need later, allowing the tiny woman to dress in her trademark brocade half-jacket and matching corset, without thirty kilos of gear hunching her over.

It made an interesting symmetry, as Matthias turned back to the scene before him. The two women dressed like dandies, with the three men in more serious attire. He had a suit with a vest and longcoat, while the two men just wore rough jackets and desert pants.

But then, the women were more important, except for him.

Matthias counted the seconds until the new car impacted with *Postmaster Seventeen*.

"Now," he said simply.

His team was just inside a fire door that Red had disarmed, in darkness deep enough that nobody would see them. He rose quickly and began walking at a deliberate pace, just exactly as the plan had called for.

Impact.

All eyes would automatically turn to look at *Postmaster Seventeen* at the eruption of noise, before returning to their business. Distractions could not be allowed when you had this many tons of rolling stock moving around, especially since the lighting in here was dim at best.

Postmaster Seventeen had moved almost exactly to the place his calculations had predicted. Matthias allowed himself a brief smile, smothering it again quickly.

He was at the second cargo car, the one that would normally be in the middle of a threesome, which was, of course, always the best place to be. Even the addition of a fourth just made things more exciting.

Postmaster Seventeen was halted.

Poised.

The noise of the rail yard doors opening filled the air.

The great doors that protected Levin from storms were immense and noisy, cutting off all conversation until they were done moving. The sudden light would also be blinding to anyone looking at it, and the event would again draw all eyes, just as joining a new car to this train had been.

Time. Perfectly.

Matthias grabbed the ladder between cars and pulled himself up to the level of the interior flooring. He pulled a key from his other pocket, opposite the watch, and stuck it into the emergency door.

The lock surrendered and Matthias pushed the door inward, slipping into the cargo car and stepping to one side. Lefty was there a moment later, drawing both pistols and standing perpendicular to the car, with a hand pointed each direction, just in case something was wrong and someone was about to step out.

Red emerged and took up a spot at his side, out of the way as Pedro pushed her gear bag across the floor and climbed in.

Lonagan came last, moving with uncommon silence and grace for a man that size.

Matthias closed the door and locked it again as they waited in the dimness, broken only by the emergency lights.

Everyone found a spot to settle and relaxed. Even Lefty holstered one of her guns, keeping her trademarked left pistol in her lap as she sat and seemed to meditate on whatever killers like that woman did, in between trigger pulls.

So far, so good. His plan had been calculated to the second, in order to get them here. After a moment, the train itself began to lurch as the engine began dragging this extra-heavy beast out into the terrible heat and wind.

Now, they waited. He would need time for the train to get away from Levin. They wouldn't even start work until they were beyond Olanchas, although he had been assured that there was nothing in cars two or three that needed anyone to access it, as car one was the mail for Olanchas and three and four were reserved for Jacumba.

After Olanchas, they would get into the fourth car and crack open a safe.

Oh, and he had a man to kill.

CHAPTER 4

Duff had started lunch while Acheson supervised the crews emptying out Car One and replacing it with more cargo headed south. Wasn't much, from what Duff had seen, but Olanchas had never been one of the bigger mountain fortresses. Not like Levin and Jacumba.

The other seven collectively only had about twice the population of either of the two biggest sisters.

He'd heard stories of larger cities, carved deep into the mountains well to the east across the great deserts, but only a crazy few travelers ever even attempted that journey. Before the Scour, legend said that there had been trains that could fly in the air at hundreds of kilometers per hour, crossing the desert in half a day.

He wasn't sure he believed it, but he'd seen strange ruins in the distance while he'd worked the line. Things nobody could explain. Leftover cities just exposed to the Scour for centuries, torn and twisted now into hideous wrecks.

There were people who lived out there all the time. Scavengers. He supposed that they had clickers that warned them if the radiation was bad enough to burn you. Plus whatever else someone might need to survive out there for longer than a week.

He'd never even considered it. Line work was out for a few days and then home again.

What did those people do for food? You couldn't eat anything that grew wild, animal or plant. Not if you wanted to live for long. Levin had covered over a whole box canyon with a dome, as well as the domes up on the plateau, just so cattle and alpacas could be raised with grains, along with vegetables and stuff from the underground hydroponic vaults. The meat was a luxury to anyone but the SkyFolk. Leather as well. And alpaca cloth was worth today what silk had supposedly been, once upon a time, from some story he barely remembered as a kid.

Like most of the Undercity, Duff made do with good, old-fashioned polyester refined from the deep wells. You could turn it into almost everything, from cloth fibers to the armor on his vest and the guns he normally wore.

What had it been like in the ancient times, when everything was made out of steel and copper, rather than just those things that had to stay inside, insulated against the Scour?

He shrugged. As much of this train as could be was a polymer of some sort, the ancient wisdom hard won from the Scour and handed down to the modern era.

Lunch was vat-burgers with cheese, something presumably easy enough that even a kid still in his teens could figure out and cook for the old man. The crews were closing up car one as he put lunch onto a pair of plates and headed forward. He grabbed a vacuum flask of the cold tea he'd made this morning and met Acheson just coming in from outside.

Olanchas had a covered spur for the mail trains, a little dogleg where switchers ran you through a door just big enough for a Postmaster train, into a long bay carved out of an overhang.

Hotter than being fully indoors, where the vast mass of the overhead mountain kept you cool, but not as bad or unsafe as just unloading things in the open.

Duff sat the plates down on the slide-out trays and watched as they opened the bay door at the far end.

"All set?" Acheson asked.

Duff dutifully buckled up his harness like a newbie then poured himself some tea before handing Acheson the flask.

"All set," Duff replied.

Fireman. Day one. Learn your job by doing it all correctly.

"You'll do, kid," Acheson smiled.

Duff fought hard not to roll his eyes, then gave up and did it anyway. It was like he was back on the line gang as a gandy dancer, sixteen, dumb as a rock, and never going to complete a formal education, so Thorstein had taken him out of school and signed him up for the union.

Hadn't turned out all that bad. Except for the recent parts.

Postmaster Seventeen lurched into motion slowly, churning those wheels beneath them as friction overcame inertia and they started rolling.

They emerged into the harsh light of early afternoon. Scars on the desert floor below them supposedly represented cities that had been destroyed in ancient times, when one Scour after another came down and killed anything with metal, leaving the survivors to mostly starve.

Duff ate in silence and just studied things. He'd never been south of Olanchas. His agency only covered the space between Olanchas this way and South Lake to the north.

Wasn't all that different from the places he knew. Hotter, but they were coming down out of the mountains and skirting the edge of the valley, with Sequoia on the right and Death somewhere on the left across the way behind the haze and dust. Aptly named, since it was supposedly hundreds of meters below sea level, if the angry tides could ever break though at Joshua and flood the high deserts east of Apple.

Duff wondered if they'd have to lay a new track to Jacumba if that happened. The valleys west of there were hot enough to make a clicker stutter, and supposedly the big engine *City of Angels* was named for a place that the angry seas had claimed for their own, down in the basin the maps showed in blood red.

He didn't seen any evidence of scavengers out here, but you never did. Just heard stories of folks. Maybe occasionally saw movement in the heat mirage, but them folks kept their distance from line teams and trains.

Did they trade with the nine cities? He'd never even considered it, but what was today, except a new start?

Duff finished his burger and decided that maybe this was just Day One of his retirement, after he'd gone another three years and could draw his twenty-five.

"Hey, Acheson," he asked out of the blue, "how long do you have left? And what will you do then?"

"Got three years until I hit my forty anniversary," the old man said with a gleam in his eye. "They'll make me quit when I'm sixty-two anyway, so I figure to only stay around until I'm sixty and call it good. Grandkids will start having their own pretty soon. Gonna spoil them something rotten. I'm a widower these last three years, so got nothing much else to do if I can't drive a train. You?"

Duff shrugged and thought about it, unbuckling and standing to clean everything.

"Was kinda thinking the same way as you," he said. "Had planned to be on the line until they made me stop, or I got too old to do it anymore. I'll be forty-one when I hit my twenty-five, and I'm pretty sure I won't be able to find any job with the union the day after that."

"What did you do, anyway?" Acheson asked. "Heard the scuttlebutt, but not the truth."

"You probably don't want to know the truth, Acheson," Duff countered gruffly.

"Try me."

"Let's just say a line foreman and his skipbosses were sending folks out into the field with equipment so old it should have been sent back to the refinery," Duff said. "And they were padding the teams out with ghost gandy dancers. Found out when someone asked me about equipment that shouldn't have been drawn. That turned into a thread I had to tug on."

"Why didn't they fire the foreman?" Acheson pressed.

"Didn't stop with her," Duff said. "Couple of union officials were in on it, across several teams. They tried to buy me off. When that didn't work, they wanted to fire me."

"But they'd have had to show cause," Acheson completed the thought with an evil smile.

"You got it," Duff smiled back. "Being Thorstein's kid helped, as the old man still has a lot of friends. Not sure how many people would have ended up getting arrested, if push came to shove. Probably some of the SkyFolk as well, since you had to have owners and factory managers involved, skimming off gear and payrolls. Made them a deal."

"They gonna be upset, you talking to me?" Acheson's voice took on an edge.

"Man bitching about corrupt union bosses?" Duff laughed. "Like I'd be the first? And you asked."

"Well, true," Acheson nodded. "A story as old as the cities."

"Plus, they leave me alone for three years, and I won't testify. Simple as that."

"So you didn't answer my question, kid," Acheson said. "What do you do with the second half of your life?"

"Damned if I know, Acheson," Duff replied. "All I know is the line. Plus what I can learn on the rails. After that, I'll have a good enough pension coming in that I could maybe travel. Ride *City of Angels* as a guest, you know. Maybe I'll take all that poker we play around the campfire and turn myself into a professional gambler. Something."

"Kid, they'll clean you out in a heartbeat," Acheson laughed. "Them folks is serious about their play."

Duff shrugged. He had three years to sort it out.

Fireman. Day One.

He went back to start his cleanup.

CHAPTER 5

Red stirred from her meditation as the train emerged from the yard at Olanchas and started the long run down to Olanchas. Matthias rose next to her.

Lefty had been poised across the way from her, tucked in behind a heavy box with both pistols in hand, probably horny at the possibility that someone would need to get into this car during the stop where she could shoot them.

Everyone had been hidden, but any door opening would have probably started a gunfight. Lefty lived for that sort of thing.

Red preferred quiet.

Pedro had slung her pack across his shoulders and waited for her like a patient burro. Lefty was up near the front of the car, covering the door into the main part of the train. Matthias and Lonagan stood off to one side.

Matthias had a contact that had gotten them the one emergency key, but the interior doors all had different locks on them. Individual, so that one person couldn't just break into every car and steal everything. Somewhere, there was a master key, stashed supposedly in a safe in the room the Postmaster had to himself in the living car behind the engine, but getting to it risked running into the engineer or his assistants.

Unnecessary, when people like her were available.

Red squatted down and studied the door leading out of this car. It had a small vestibule on the other side, where a similar structure from any next car would form a petite room with a soft seal. Enough to keep wind and grit out, if not sound or heat.

There was nothing visible on this side of the door, but she'd spent enough time in jails to appreciate looking for alarms where they weren't supposed to be. She'd still be there, if Matthias hadn't come along, needing an expert.

She popped her knuckles loudly inside her fingerless gloves and turned the switch on the deadbolt, letting the movement itself tell her about the innards. If she really wanted to, she could have taken the entire handle and lock apart, but she was familiar with the model. All train cars used locks supplied by the same company, and pinned by one of only three union locksmiths.

Pain in the ass, but at least predictable.

She reached into one of her belt pouches and pulled out her picks and her half-glasses.

Getting older was a pain in the ass, if thirty-one was old, but Red's eyes had never been that great in the first place, so she had a pair of lenses no taller than her thumbs, set in a polymer frame that had been painted to look like brass.

Not that she actually needed them to pick locks. That was a job for touch and muscle memory. The sort of thing you could do in complete darkness or blindfolded.

Still, they calmed her as she rested them down on the tip of her button nose and took a breath.

Behind her, Lefty wore a leather, two-gun rig with paired

revolvers and individual cartridges around the back. No other gear besides death.

Red was the one with a dozen individual pouches, all containing the various little things she needed, from a lubricating oil to freshen balky locks, to a glass vial with an acid strong enough to just eat all the pins if she was feeling destructive and had time to kill.

They had time, but leaving destruction in her wake was an amateur move. Let them spend all that time trying to figure out what she'd done, without even a scratch left behind.

Red moved out into the little pocket between cars now and tested the air. Gonna be hot today, but not hot enough that she wanted to strip down some layers. That was another amateur move. Work how you feel most comfortable, even if that included matching brocade corset and half-jacket in royal blue and black, plus dark gray jodhpurs and lace-up boots.

Red was a misnomer anyway. She chuckled to herself as she knelt and started to study the next lock. Her hair was black, with gray coming in above both ears like men did. Pale blue eyes.

There was generally nothing at all red about her, except her given name, prominent on wanted posters across the nine cities. Amelia Zhu. Last name was ancient, supposedly a Chinese term that translated into modern as *Vermilion*, or, in her case *Red*. Most folks didn't even know what vermilion was.

Same lock here. Same locksmith. Made sense, since *Postmaster Seventeen* was the engine, the crew car, and these three cargo cars. It was only that fourth car that would be a real pain her ass. The magic one that held the prize Matthias had broken her out of jail to help him steal.

Red worked methodically. The train rumbled and swayed as it crossed rails and turned along curves, and she had to hold every pin as she got it aligned. Even a sneeze right now and she'd have to start over.

Amateur move.

Six pins. Six depths. Pain in the ass. Needed a pro to pick something this complicated.

Fortunately, Matthias had hired her. Took longer than she expected, but Red put that down to patience and the train swaying as it came over a lip and started down a long valley.

Not nerves.

Never with Red.

The lock surrendered. The handle turned.

Red rose and pushed the door in, stepping out of the heat and into the third car. She had been expecting Pedro to be right behind her, but she decided that she really wasn't surprised when it was Lefty.

There might be people in here needed killing.

Red managed to not roll her eyes as the woman slithered past her into the car and poked her nose and barrels into every space that might hold a rail cop. Red just stood off to one side as Matthias came next, then Pedro, and Lonagan at the end.

She closed the door behind the big man and set the lock, just to slow someone down if they had somehow detected anything and were headed back to check it out. There were no alarms on this side of the door, nor unexplained wires emerging, so she presumed that it was fine.

Still, they were facing the fourth car.

She signaled Pedro to turn around so she could get at her gear. Inside, she pulled out the pistol she preferred, hooking the holster to her utility belt and tying the lanyards around her thigh.

She drew the weapon and smiled. Matthias had managed to break into the evidence room and steal all her gear back for her, too, so she had the antique, breech-loading single-shot that had belonged to her grandmother. Like Lefty, a row of individual cartridges on a belt she hooked to her belt below the pouches.

This pistol was mostly wood, from a cache of old maple that some explorer had salvaged somewhere a century ago. The barrel and trigger were polymer, with only the hammer and firing mechanism made of metal.

One shot at a time, unlike Lefty, but it gave Red extra piece of mind, just in case Matthias's contact had been lying about there being nobody in that last car.

She already knew the whole thing was an inside job, but had to trust Matthias that it wasn't a setup to send her back to prison.

The next time would probably be forever, given her arrest history. Some folks had no sense of humor about those things.

She waited until Matthias and Lefty were satisfied with everything in the third car. They were surrounded by bags of mail and boxes of stuff being shipped, but none of it had any intrinsic value, unless you already knew which box to look in.

Red doubted that car three had anything. That was the whole reason someone had added a special car today.

Red settled a put upon sigh as she waited.

Matthias eventually returned, Lefty in his wake.

"You ready?" he asked in that superior tone that he did when he wanted to make a point.

Red refused to rise to his bait. He already had Lefty. More than one woman was just being greedy. Even if he was rather handsome in a dark, enigmatic way when he wanted to be.

She'd seen enough of him when he forgot to be charming. Lefty just didn't care.

"Been waiting for you folks to clear out of my way," Red smiled up at the two of them.

Grandmother had taught her that smile. Usually accompanied by her favorite saying. "Isn't that precious?" with enough sneer to put someone into their place more or less permanently.

Red didn't go for the jugular today. She wanted to be rich first.

Matthias bowed his head amiably and stepped to one side, grandly gesturing for her to precede him. Red kept her snarl to herself.

Nerves. Nothing more.

She just didn't like the way Lefty eyed her when the woman didn't think poor Red was paying any attention.

Back to what was usually the last door on the back of the train, but like all the others it could be attached to others, so she opened it and stepped into the vestibule, smelling Lefty right behind her by the perfume the woman wore.

Red knelt and studied that last lock. Looked standard. Car had looked standard enough, from the quick view she'd gotten as Matthias snuck them all across the yard in the darkness.

Suddenly, she was happy to have the killer lurking over one shoulder.

Matthias had been given inside information. Who was supposed to burn on this one?

Red set her picks and began to work. She could feel those two revolvers aimed over her head, in case someone suddenly opened the door to confront them.

At this range, the bullets would probably catapult the stupid bastard back into the middle of the train, and whatever ambush had been set up for them.

Red glanced to her left over her glasses, through a small gap in the join between cars. Desert outside. Down in that long valley somewhere, headed to where the ocean had crept up the shore over the centuries and reclaimed so many of the ruins of what had been the world, once upon a time.

There were folks crazy enough to strap on air tanks and dive down into that space, looking for ancient treasure, but there were also stories about things that had decided to take over, once humans were out of the way. And no longer sailing those dangerous oceans.

She shivered and went back to her lock. She could control this part of the world, if nothing else.

And she had killers and masterminds to deal with rail police and wild animals, if it came to that.

Lock felt the same. Another six-and-six. More recently lubricated than Seventeen's had been, but Red figured that this car had been mostly in storage, pulled out for special runs like this, rather than being out in the heat and grit.

Didn't go any faster, but that was her taking her time.

And slipped once and losing four pins with a snarl that would have made grandfather blush. Had, when grandmother had uttered it once.

"Problems?" Lefty asked serenely.

No, bitch. Occupational hazards.

But she didn't say that. Using her outside voice, anyway.

Red grunted and started over, not even giving the woman the success of getting under her skin.

Much.

CHAPTER 6

Lefty could see why Matthias had decided to rescue this particular Ice Princess from her dragon-guarded tower, given his pick of all the thieves in Levin he could have gone after.

Gorgeous, in a petite, compact way. Smart, when so many of them were skilled, but about as dumb as a box of rocks. Competent but quiet about it, rather than bragging all the time. You almost forgot she was here if she wasn't talking.

Lefty didn't do books all that much, beyond sword and sorcery and good bodice-rippers that let her exist in a place where her fantasies could push as many envelopes as possible, regardless of ethics, history, morals, or gymnastic ability.

Honestly, Matthias was fun in bed, if a little boring and predictable sometimes. Red hadn't shown any interest in joining them, or Lefty might have made a pass at the woman, just to see what the Ice Princess was like if you got her out of all that lovely brocade and down to vulnerable flesh.

Still, not having competition for Matthias meant she didn't have to watch the woman. At least not like that.

Maybe after all this, she and the Ice Princess could find a different way to have a professional partnership. She snickered to herself, quiet, so that the others didn't hear. To the rest of them, she was just a gunman. A stone killer who dressed nice and wore pretty hats, but could still outdraw any man and shoot him dead if he decided not to take no for an answer.

It had been a long time since that had happened. Not since she'd started sleeping with a pistol under her pillow when she was fourteen.

This train job was going to make her rich. Even her share was supposedly more money than Lefty had ever seen in her life in one place. Even the biggest pots in the craziest poker game she had ever watched.

Matthias didn't do poker. He liked his odds predictable, his grifts solid, his safes easy to crack.

Easy enough, anyway, with the Ice Princess along to handle that part. Lefty would just have to protect them all against rail cops with friendly hands and wagging tongues.

She tapped the barrels together for luck. Silently, because Red had already lost her concentration once and they didn't really have all day to do this. Well, technically they did, since they only had to have it done in time to get off the train at their stop and send the driver on his way.

But that was hours yet. Matthias always believed in getting things done as fast as possible so there was time to just lay around and relax.

Outside of bed, that was a great way to approach life, but it did have its drawbacks in certain situations. Maybe she'd need to hire herself a poolboy to take care of those needs, when she was so rich that she didn't need Matthias around anymore?

Ice Princess did her thing as Lefty watched. Only screwed up once more, which was two better than Lefty had been expecting. After three, there would have been some razor-sharp teasing, because at that point, they could have just blown the damned lock apart with some explosives or something and been done with it.

But it wasn't her gig. Matthias had set it up.

Or been set up into it. Lefty wasn't sure. And Matthias wasn't one for pillow talk. Doubly so, since he tended to just roll over and fall asleep like a boy when he was done. No, he just considered her muscle.

Well, boobs and muscle. Like Ice Princess, he could have found himself any number of other gunslingers, but they wouldn't look nearly as good in a leather corset top over her billowy, white shirt. The mostly-backless kind with the leather front chopped out to circle her breasts, while still strapping tight around her waist and emphasizing her neck.

She'd pulled out her slate-gray bowler today for this run. It just *made* the outfit, in subtle and distracting ways. Especially when Ice Princess was wearing a loud pattern that looked like it should have been made into a couch, bright blue swirling with black, both bolero and corset underneath.

Ice Princess was done. Reached up at hand and turned the handle smoothly.

Lefty automatically thumbed both hammers back and centered the door. She really only had one official purpose here, beyond keeping Matthias entertained in ways that the others couldn't or wouldn't handle.

Guns aimed, she nodded down to Red and the woman pressed the door in as Lefty stared down the twin barrels, looking for movement.

Nothing.

Not a complete surprise, but might have been.

Lefty stepped around Red and shouldered the door the rest of the way until it hit the wall solid, one pistol trailing it as if someone was going to be standing there to be shot.

Same interior as the other two cars, with shelves at shoulder level and space for boxes and bags below that.

Except that there weren't any. Just a big, black safe standing opposite the loading door and backed up against the side.

Lefty slid to her left and kept both guns on the spot she couldn't see, just beyond the monstrous safe.

She wasn't left-handed. That wasn't where the name came from, although she generally did nothing to dissuade that talk. Her real name was Harper Solak. The name Solak was Turkish, according to her mom, and meant *left-handed*, so apparently one of dad's ancestors, back in the old world, had been just as big a misfit weirdo as his however-many-times removed granddaughter.

Empty carriage. Just that safe, big enough that she, Matthias, and Ice Princess could have had a quickie inside, if there weren't any shelves to get in the way.

She nodded back at the others and holstered her rig with a quick twirl to let both hammers down softly.

Red was in first, but slid to the side like she did, getting out of the way emotionally as well as physically. Matthias was right behind her, then the two mutts that were just along as strong backs.

Lefty wondered if they were actually getting a share of the whole, or just a straight fee. Wasn't like either of them weren't interchangeable with a hundred other thieves and cutthroats.

But then, she and Red were, too, so maybe she shouldn't look so down her nose at the others. At least not until she was so rich she never had to put on guns again and could live her life in a succession of alpaca-hair robes, dyed with only the most expensive inks.

Yeah, one last job, then she'd be free of all these bozos and could find someone more entertaining in bed.

She watched Matthias as he studied the safe. Didn't feel like a double cross on his part. She couldn't help it if someone else was double-crossing them, except to make sure that the first twelve went down bleeding to death while she ducked for cover and reloaded.

Lefty moved the rear corner of the car and settled her butt against the cool plastic surface while she waited for something that needed killing.

The day was young.

CHAPTER 7

Matthias sized up the situation with a quick glance. Just as he'd been told it would be. Empty carriage, save for the safe. A load of gold coins inside destined for a bank in Jacumba, something about adjusting trade flows that hadn't made any sense when it had been explained to him, so Matthias had just nodded at the time.

Everything was insured against lost, which included train robbers pulling off the boldest, most daring caper in a century.

"Lonagan, close and lock the door," he ordered the big man, watching just long enough to make sure the man was listening.

He turned to Red and studied the woman. He knew that Lefty saw her as potential competition, but he doubted that the woman was. Nobody even knew if she liked boys in the way Lefty did, or even women. Certainly, she'd spent enough time in women's prisons to have developed the taste, but he hadn't asked.

It wasn't pertinent to his needs. All that mattered was that she wouldn't double-cross him, because the next time she was arrested, Red was going to be locked away forever, and not just as an escaped convict, but as a career, *habitual* criminal.

Even telling the authorities everything she knew at that point wouldn't change anything. At best, she'd only serve twenty years until they decided that maybe she'd learned a lesson.

"Red?" he asked simply, stepping back.

Matthias made sure that he also wasn't in Lefty's way if she had to suddenly draw and fire at someone opening the far door. Most likely, she would be shooting right over Red's head at that point, so hopefully the other woman knew to fall flat at gunfire, instead of standing up and getting shot.

The plan was executing perfectly. He checked his watch. They were even about ten minutes ahead of schedule, which would be a useful gain against friction later.

Always friction. Foolish burglars and thieves assumed perfect timing bringing everything together, and blew everything when a guard had to stop and tie a loose shoelace or take a piss, throwing him ten seconds off some artificial schedule.

Luck had been with Matthias that time, but it also hadn't been his job, so when the guard started shooting, he'd been just another young punk off in a corner, watching someone else's gig go south before madly running for his life and managing to get away.

Still, the lessons stayed with him.

Red knelt in front of the safe like a priestess communing with her Goddess. The only thing that would make the image more perfect would be if she was nude doing it, like the ancients had done, but he wasn't going to suggest it.

She wasn't part of his gang. Or at least hadn't been for long. Matthias wasn't sure the gang would survive if they really hit a jackpot of coin here, as greed would come into play after that.

It always did.

But Lonagan was a simple man, content to hide his take in a mattress and slowly drink himself to death over years. And Pedro wasn't much smarter than the burro he was impersonating. That might be a problem later, when he might speak the wrong words, but Matthias had plans to make it look like a tragic accident in ways that couldn't be traced back.

Lefty was likely to split. Red would vanish as well.

And Matthias Torosyan would simply cease to exist, with a new name, a new wardrobe, and maybe a new address.

Hell, he might even make his way back to the Nine Cities at some point, just because he could. Whatever the others did would be their own choice, once they could no longer implicate him, or the folks that had contacted him and set up this job.

They didn't even care that much about the gold. Just wanted a man dead. The safe was his payment for plausible deniability on their part later.

Red had Pedro set her bag down. The man retreated to a corner and sat, back against the side wall and legs bent. Lonagan joined him a moment later, placing both of them horribly out of position if something went wrong.

He glanced over at Lefty, just to confirm her semi-sneer at the other two men.

Yes, she was prepared to cover them and kill anyone happening along.

Matthias relaxed.

Red had a stethoscope out now. Instead of a key lock, this demonic coffin had a wheel on the front, with one hundred and twenty little white hashes around the rim.

She turned the thing counter-clockwise a number of times, pausing at one point to pull a plastic bottle of something and spray it into the top edge of the wheel and then start spinning again.

Machine oil. Lubricant, from the smell that suddenly filled the room. He only noticed because the rest of the space had been the smell of bodies that hadn't showered recently enough. That would be Lonagan and Pedro. Both of the women were fastidious about that. There might not be interesting food when you lived in the Undercity's underworld, but water was cheap and showers and soap a given.

Maybe he'd go back to grifting after this, just so he could spend time around wealthy people who bathed religiously and spent time in the sun, under the domes where you could turn golden-brown in safety. Poor people either lived underground and faded to white, or worked in the sun all the time and turned as dark brown.

Red leaned forward, as though invoking her Goddess, one hand turning the dial while the other held her auditory icon against the metal and listened for guidance.

Or something. Benefit of a classical education, and all that, but at times like this it filled him with jokes that nobody around him was sophisticated enough to grasp. Lefty read trash and romances. Red didn't read, as far as he had been able to tell. Matthias wasn't even sure Lonagan and Pedro *could* read. It wasn't generally a useful skill, when most Undercity jobs required strong backs or nimble hands, rather than brains.

He occasionally felt left out as a result.

Still, she worked quickly, trying various things until she suddenly nodded to herself.

Matthias had no idea how one cracked a safe, so he concentrated on the mesmerizing movements of the thief instead, slowly seducing the safe into giving itself up under her patient ministrations, caressing and twisting things so carefully, while still listening to every breath, every movement, like the machine had a safe word it might mutter when things got to be too much.

Back and forth she twisted that knob with sure fingers. Turning to the left until she was satisfied. Back to the right, but not as many times, as though the demon's breath was catching.

Back again now, one whole twist until she delicately adjusted things with just the tips of her fingers around the inner wheel of the dial.

Yes, there. She paused, left go her own breath, and turned the knob slowly clockwise until it suddenly came to rest with a click. Matthias blew out his breath and wondered if anyone else needed a smoke at this point.

She reached up and wrapped those strong fingers firmly around the handle, giving it a good, solid pull with a thump that echoed across the space. The door moved, just a little, but she held it in place while her other hand pulled the stethoscope down around her neck and she rose.

Pedro and Lonagan both stirred, but neither moved from their spot in the corner.

Lefty did move now, drawing one pistol and holding it in an off-hand way that told Matthias she could lift it and fire so fast that nobody else would be able to react.

That was why he had hired her, after all. The rest was just frosting he got to lick off his fingers.

Red looked back over her shoulder at him and Matthias nodded, his own breath catching with the excitement of the moment.

The thief stepped backwards and drew the safe door with her and then to one side.

Inside, the safe was lined on three sides with shelves starting about thigh-high and going all the way above his head. The center was open, where a man could stand inside if he wished and reach all the way to the back of the shelves.

Most of the space was empty today, as he had known it would be. But there was a box at the bottom. Two decimeters deep. Three tall. Nearly a meter wide. Wrought in a hard, gray plastic that conveyed incredible durability, just watching.

On the outside, markings from Levin Industrial Treasury. The Bank of Levin, itself. The place where everyone had an account opened on the day they were born and everything they ever made was deposited.

If they were legitimate citizens.

Matthias felt his breath catch again.

"Lonagan, Pedro," he called hoarsely, pointing at the interior of the safe.

They moved now, rising and lumbering over. Red moved back against a wall while Lefty had everyone covered, both those coming into the room as well as those already inside.

This would be where the first double-cross from the inside might unfold, but he was sure he had picked these people well. Plus, they were still on a moving train, and didn't know where they were supposed to get off.

It wasn't like they could just hop off at Olanchas when they arrived, and expect that nobody would notice.

Lonagan reached in those long arms and grabbed the handle at this end. He grunted as he pulled it to the threshold, then moved inside to the space cleared. Pedro grabbed the handle when Lonagan moved and the two of them lifted it heavily outside, cursing quietly as they did.

If his contact wasn't lying, there were fifty kilograms of gold inside there. Almost fifteen hundred coins, minted to the standard the ancients had called a troy ounce and just perfect to sit in the palm of his hand when he closed his fingers around it.

"Red?" he gestured for her to come back to the center as Lonagan turned the box sideways to reveal a simple padlock through the far end.

She approached warily, watching his eyes as much as the room. Interestingly, she almost completely ignored Lefty and the two men. She hadn't been able to read his mind as he watched her work, had he?

But no, this was just exceptional wariness on her part.

Waiting for that other shoe to drop.

He could understand that, but Matthias had no plans to do anything wrong by this woman. She was about to make him filthy, stinking rich. Herself as well, but he'd never have to see her again once they got to Sanctuary and bought their way inside.

She knelt again, sideways so that the men were all in front of her and Lefty out of sight.

Interesting, the unconscious movements that betray our inner selves.

She studied the lock and drew out her picks again. Thrusting them delicately inside, she began probing for that spot that would make everything light up happily and then surrender.

Matthias remembered to breathe again as the mechanism popped itself open.

Red pulled the padlock and slipped it into her bag, possibly as a trophy, then pushed the lid to one side. Satisfied, she rose and moved to the side.

Matthias stepped up now and studied the cloth bags revealed inside, a heavy, quilted polyester wrapped tight around columns of coins thrust rudely into the air. There were five of them, each bulging with weight.

He opened the bag on top and reached in, wrapping his hands firmly around the cylinder inside and letting the girth and mass convey happy thoughts as he pulled it out.

"Pedro, hold out your hand," he ordered, turning to the man.

Pedro did, after a moment of hesitation as the words took time to filter into that dense brain of his.

Each stack of coins was wrapped in paper like a smooth prophylactic. Matthias opened one end so he could spill them out, working the shaft of the coins with both hands to get it empty.

Gold coins stained Pedro's hands when Matthias was done. Thirty of them, although Pedro had dropped three. Red caught them as they started to bounce and roll, adding them back to the pile.

The smiles around the room were enough to lit the darkness, were night to fall on them.

"Now what?" Red asked, looking up at him not with innocence, but perhaps innocent concern.

He had told her only the vague parts, as her part of this operation was technically complete and all she had to do now was accompany them to their destination, where he'd pay everyone off and probably never see them again.

"Pedro, put them back," he pointed at the box and stepped back as the man somehow managed to slip them all back into the larger bag that had held them.

"We taking this now?" Pedro asked, hands on the large box.

"Not yet," Matthias said, tapping his jacket where the letter with his instructions and details waited. "There's still one thing we need to do."

CHAPTER 8

The afternoon was getting long when Duff got the cleaning done in the kitchen, more tea made, and headed back up to the engine.

"Okay, fireman," Acheson said gamely. "Time for your first lesson."

Duff was buckled in and watching. Acheson didn't look like he had moved in hours.

"This is a deadman switch," Acheson pointed to the throttle he had been holding. "As long as I'm pushing it forward, the train will continue to move. If I let go for longer than two seconds, it will snap back to the rest position and cut current to the wheels. Eventually, the whole train will slow down and then the brakes will lock in place."

Duff nodded sagely. Or something.

"Speed is controlled by this dial here," Acheson pointed. "And shown on this gauge. All you do is keep the deadman forward. Grab yours and move it forward until it clicks."

Duff looked at his setup, a mirror image of Acheson's. He grabbed the joystick and pushed it forward. There was a little resistance, but not much. He could see developing a certain muscle if he had to hold this for a career, but he had muscles from the line.

"Good," Acheson nodded. "Next, study the lay of the bed itself in front of you. I'm always scanning the near and distant horizons for obstacles that are cutting our right of way, like a landslide or maybe some wild animal big enough that the cowcatcher up front has issues. Seen a few, but nothing this far south. The big beasts tend to be at the north end."

"Like?" Duff asked.

"Moose or elk," Acheson answered. "Not one, but maybe a whole herd wanders onto the bed and can't move fast enough. Around here, you might sneak up on a camel too stupid to run. At least the elephants are smart enough to understand what that rumble means. They'll move the whole herd off to one side and just watch us go by."

"Elephants?" Duff asked. "Like those things from Africa?"

"You got it, kid," Acheson smiled. "Couple herds of them up north, roaming around. Nobody knows where they come from, but all the old records say they aren't from around here."

"Huh."

Duff glanced over at movement and realized the Acheson had let go of his deadman switch and pulled it all the way back to rest. The engine was still going though.

"So now you're driving, Duff," Acheson said. "Most of what I do is just sit here and think quiet thoughts as I drive. I know a few men compose music. Others write novels in their head, sometimes writing them down in between runs. You got to have something to keep your mind from falling into ruts and spiraling down in on itself, understand?"

"Yeah." Duff said. "Probably useful advice if I was going to be doing this for long, but three years isn't going to even make me into a secondman, let alone an engineer like you."

"Maybe," Acheson agreed. "But we were talking earlier about what you do with yourself after those three years are up. Man's got to have hobbies. Known too many who didn't. Got to that retirement date, went home, and sat down in the living room to watch the vid. Most of them were dead within six months. Ran out of things to do, and remembering to stay alive was one of them."

"I hear you," Duff retorted. "But not a problem I have to solve today."

"Not today, youngster, no," Acheson agreed. "But damned soon, because eventually tomorrow turns into never if you aren't paying attention. Don't miss out, thinking you have forever. Even at your age, you'll run out before you expect it."

Duff shrugged. He didn't disagree with the old man, but six weeks ago he'd still been a respected Senior Lineman. Everything since then had been a whirlwind of private meetings, threats, bribes, and investigations.

None of it had ever emerged from under the mountain, and wouldn't as long as everyone played nice, but he was still trying to find his footing.

"So now, I'm going to go pee," Acheson suddenly unbuckled himself and rose. "You'll be fine for the two minutes I'm gone. This is a long flat with visibility for several miles. If you see anything bad, just let go of the switch. If you snap it all the way back hard, the emergency brakes will also engage, but we've got a lot of mass to stop, so it will take time to get there. You good?"

"So far," Duff replied.

So far.

Acheson smiled and crossed the cab to put a friendly hand on Duff's shoulder, but didn't say anything.

Duff just stared out the front window and wondered what the hell he was going to do next.

Any next.

CHAPTER 9

Red followed the others forward. Most of the others. Pedro was still behind her like a faithful puppy, hauling all her gear in a big satchel that weighed more than half as much as she did.

Lefty was leading. Correction, Lefty's pistols were leading, with the crazy woman a step behind them. Matthias followed her. Lonagan was so big that Red couldn't see anything around the man most of the time.

Forward.

Something about hijacking the train now and holding the crew hostage until Matthias got to where he needed to go so everyone could get off.

At that point, the other half of his plan would come into play, but she was wearing clothing designed for the heat of the desert and could carry a lot of water.

At least her boots were sturdy enough to make a hike, and comfortable doing it, all heavy enough to protect her against sand and poisonous things.

Car three hadn't changed, but got searched quickly by the gunslinger anyway. Same with two and one. Paranoia, but Red did appreciate that the woman didn't cut any corners.

In cracking safes and picking locks, you couldn't do that either. It would fail, or maybe you'd end up blowing up your treasure to bits. Or yourself.

Red never cut corners, either. The times she'd been in prison had been on account of other people talking too much and getting themselves arrested.

No honor among thieves. Dumb ones, anyway.

She had her doubts about Lonagan and Pedro. Matthias said he had a plan for them. Hopefully, it didn't include the psycho chick just shooting them, because it was only a short step after that to making sure Red never talked, either.

She put one hand carefully onto the butt of her pistol. She'd only get one shot if she had to use it, but that would be Matthias if this turned into a double-cross.

Lefty would put her down a moment later, but that woman wasn't a mastermind. Just a killer. It would be automatic.

The woman might even shoot him first, if Matthias really was up to no good. Hopefully Red would still manage to get one shot off in that case.

Red didn't draw her weapon, but studied what she could see of the two leaders up front, wondering when things would get ugly.

CHAPTER 10

An electric thrill coursed through Lefty's body. Just holding both pistols, cocked and ready to deal death, carried a surge of power and emotion that nothing short of a long string of good orgasms could match. Matthias on his very best days, as it were.

They were relying on her now.

Every one of them.

The train had two crew members, according to what Matthias had supposedly been told. Engineer and an assistant of some sort.

Lefty would handle the load now. She was the only one of them good enough to just wing someone so they could take them prisoner, rather than letting someone's life bleed out on the hard, gray deck under her feet.

Forward she crept, eyeing every crevice and gap for eyes staring back. Nobody knew where the crew would be. At least one of them was forward, since the train was moving, but they hadn't made it all the way up front yet.

She doubted that it was all an elaborate trap to capture her and the rest of the crew. That was just silliness, as they could have all been arrested at Olanchas easily. Just cut the cargo cars loose from the engine when nobody was looking and surround them with enough police that they couldn't shoot their way out.

Lefty had no death wish. She'd have surrendered, rather than deciding to die in a stupid blaze of glory. Ice Princess would be the same way, unless she was hiding some terrible, dark secret from everyone, including herself. That left the boys. Matthias was the kind of man who firmly believed he could lie and spin his way out of any situation, regardless of some husband walking in while Matthias was busy fucking the wife.

She didn't hold that against him, because she'd seen the box of gold that they were all going to share. Or there would be problems.

Lonagan was dumb muscle. One with a high pain threshold, from the stories she'd heard about him. She'd put four into him, just to make sure, if it came to that. But he'd do whatever Matthias told him until then.

Pedro. Lefty had known dogs smarter than Pedro. And less loyal. She didn't have to worry about Pedro.

No, Lefty felt safe ruling out a trap and a double-cross from that direction.

They were in the car where they'd started this adventure now. Lefty took a step to her right and pivoted back to catch Red's eye.

"I need your help getting into the first car," Lefty said in a friendly tone, modulating all the emotions back down under control so she didn't scare Ice Princess any more than she already had.

Red nodded and slipped around the two men.

She had a nervous smell about her now that hadn't been around earlier. Lefty recognized it under the smell of flowers from her morning toilet. Not expensive stuff, but a quality knock-off that was almost as good and way cheaper.

What you'd find on a safe-cracker, rather than a SkyFolk call girl with the kinds of money those chicks could make for a few years if they played their cards right.

Lefty smiled at her in a commiserating way. Red was the safest one here, because her wildest dreams were all quiet and inhibited. The exact opposite of the sorts of grand gestures Matthias seemed to live for.

Red blinked up at her in surprise, as if seeing her face for the first time.

Lefty let her smile turn warm and friendly. They were all almost rich, after all.

Red opened the first door warily, peeking through, and then nodded.

Lefty followed her into the tiny space between cars, where the smell of safe-cracker seemed to get stronger.

Lefty wondered if the woman was sweating hard now, and that was triggering her perfume to work overtime.

Lefty wasn't sure what the chick had to fear. She had the most dangerous woman in the world protecting her.

Red got to work. Lefty covered her. The lock surrendered peacefully.

Lefty went through first, as always. Same sort of car as the others, almost as empty as four had been, since they'd offloaded lots at Olanchas and not put much back, at least from the sound.

Nothing in here looked worth stealing, except as a memento or something,

Still, Lefty checked. Never trust an empty room until you scope it all.

Nobody and nothing. Not even trinkets worth boosting as she went by, since she'd have to holster a pistol first.

Her and Red moved to the front of the car.

Now was when things would get interesting. This was the stage when they were getting into the places where they'd start finding the crew.

Either Red was getting the hang of these locks, or the one on the passenger car was a cheaper model, because she had it apart almost as fast as if she'd had a key for the door.

Lefty was close enough to smell her. And vice versa, but Lefty had no idea what her smell was. Clean soap without a perfume. Just a trace of lavender from the stuff she used to clean her leather, most likely. At least polymer guns didn't need a lot of lubricating oil. Nasty smell.

Red was breathing a little harshly, but it wasn't that aggressive gasp that Matthias got when he was aroused by a job. The one that sounded almost like he did in bed.

No, this was just emotion. Too keyed up, probably by Lefty being in her space.

"You're doing great," Lefty whispered too quietly for Matthias and the others to hear.

Red flinched, but seemed to relax a little, so maybe it was just nerves and nothing else.

Red opened the door handle just enough for Lefty to push, and then seemed to melt herself against the side of the space.

Lefty thrust forward with an elbow and covered the room.

Kitchen area. Breakfast nook that could seat four on one side, cooking and prep space on the other. Open in the middle and a hallway leading to the front.

Empty.

Smelled like vat-burgers had been lunch, that rich, spicy

tang you got from a veggie burger than wasn't alpaca. Like the railroad would ever serve its employees real meat.

The aroma was fading. That late, lingering stage, so they'd eaten earlier, rather than her interrupting dinner now. She'd eaten snacks and a picnic lunch packed today.

Lefty stood perfectly still in the middle of the open area, unsure why she didn't want to go any further, but willing to listen to that little voice in her belly that had an opinion.

A moment later, a door opened in the hallway in front of her. A man stepped out and goggled when he saw her.

Or her pistols. Maybe he was staring at the way her corset wrapped itself around her breasts with shape and color to call attention. Whatever it was, Lefty didn't think he'd actually seen her face.

Old man. Maybe sixty. Tall and skinny. Might weight sixty kilos, too. Stopped dead still.

She moved like a snake with a frozen rabbit, just like in the ancient stories.

"Not a word," she growled at him, close enough now that she didn't have to yell above the clatter of the wheels over the tracks below her. "Hands in the air, so I don't have to shoot you."

He complied, but it was more an automatic thing than a conscious decision on his art. One point five centimeter bores probably looked like eternity when they were pointed at you. Death as big as the night sky.

Lefty felt more than heard the others pour into the car now, but dared not take her eyes off the man she had covered.

"Who else is on the train?" she demanded in a low voice.

"Just the kid driving right now," he stammered fearfully.

"Where?"

"Duff's up in the engine," he said, nodding with his head

and one shoulder. "I need to get back up there, because he really doesn't know what he's doing. I just needed a potty break."

"Is the door to the engine locked?" she asked.

"No." He seemed surprised. Or going into shock. Something.

Lefty shifted to one side so she could see Matthias's face now. And the gun he had in his hand. Lonagan had a pistol out as well. So did Red. Only Pedro didn't but again, that wasn't a bad thing.

"Red first," Matthias said to her before turning to the old man. "You'll follow her. I don't need to kill you, so don't do anything stupid."

Lefty caught the odd emphasis in Matthias's words. He was always a stickler for linguistics, so she was surprised. Was he supposed to kill someone else? There was supposedly only one other person here.

The man was old enough to be the engineer, so he'd likely have a punk kid even younger than her as his assistant. What made a kid important enough to kill?

But she didn't ask. Didn't matter. They had the gold and enough time to carry out the rest of Matthias's plan.

Still, time to be careful. There were three other doors in this hallway, as she slid quickly around the old man and holstered a pistol to free up a hand.

She glanced into the space the old man had emerged from. Bathroom with a shower stall and a toilet. Cleaner than most men ever left theirs. Said good things about the crew on this train.

Across the hallway she opened a linen closet and smelled stale sheets washed with too much bleach too many times. And mothballs set to keep the insects from trying to eat everything.

Down on the linen closet side was a small bedroom with twin bunks. Looked abandoned. Felt that way, too. Nobody hiding inside.

Across from it was a longer room than the first one, with a single bed for the engineer, an armoire filled with clothes, and a chair. There was a bookcase next to it, so she studied the titles.

Mostly histories and biographies, from the looks of it, plus a few that might be westerns, or maybe western romances. She'd come back later and maybe steal one before she left.

The rest of the crew waited and watched her work.

Lefty paused at the door to the engine compartment. It was closed, but all day long Red had been opening doors for her, so she could have both pistols out. Felt awkward, doing it by herself.

But she did.

Twisted the knob and pushed it in, stepping into the space and drawing her pistol in one fluid motion that had her again in the middle of a large space.

Two chairs in here for drivers, one on each side and elevated like bar stools.

One on the left held a very surprised man blinking and maybe thinking about getting himself killed.

"Don't move and you won't get hurt," she ordered him curtly.

Behind her, Lefty heard the rest of her team, and the old man, moving up and into the cabin with her.

CHAPTER 11

Duff managed to not yell an obscenity when he glanced back and it was some young woman standing there instead of Acheson. For the briefest moment, he might have thought it was some sort of weird hazing thing, but she had a pistol pointed at him. One just like the revolver he had back in his bunk with the rest of his gear.

Young. Maybe a hard twenty-five, maybe younger. Porcelain skin that never went out in the sun, unlike he'd done for a living, getting all leathery in the process. Cute hat. Strange, leather top with a wide oval cut out for both breasts to poke through and a white shirt underneath that was nicer than anything he owned.

The rest of her was just as impressive. She wasn't beautiful, but had a cold beauty to her face that he could appreciate.

Menacing green eyes focused on his face, with just a hint of a smile.

Not much he could do, with one hand holding the deadman switch and properly buckled in. Nothing that wouldn't get him killed, anyway.

"So what's going on?" he asked after a long beat, with as much cool aplomb as he could manage in this situation.

He liked the way her face turned into exquisite marble as she smiled tartly, just for a ghost of a second.

"It's a train robbery," she replied, with about as much emotion as if he'd asked her the time.

Acheson appeared now, hands in the air and staggering a little as someone shoved him into the cabin. Duff could see several others back there as well.

A man with a desert-style longcoat and a pistol in one hand took up station beside the gunslinger woman. Looked to be the guy in charge, from the way he was holding himself. Shorter than the gunslinger woman and swarthy, like some of the Latinos Duff had known on the line, ancestors from the distant south, back when it was still habitable.

Two obvious thugs followed the guy, making it obvious that the short man was in charge, at least in his own mind.

A woman in a pretty blue and black outfit seemed to almost vanish into a corner as she entered.

"Should I stop the train?" Duff asked the woman with the guns.

Whatever else, she was the one issuing orders. Duff had known pistoleros in his time. Out on the rail you occasionally had to shoot things that were digging up lines, or maybe were looking to make you a snack. Duff was a fast hand with a gun, but this woman had the look of a killer in her eyes.

She turned to the short guy with a quick glance of her own, never losing track of him or Acheson, even as she slid a little sideways, covering Acheson from directly behind his seat as the old man sat down.

Duff assumed short guy was the mastermind behind whatever the hell was happening.

Them pistols never wavered once.

Duff really had no desire to die today.

"No," mastermind announced. "We're ahead of schedule, but that just means we'll be gone sooner."

"Oh, shit," Acheson whispered.

Duff's head snapped around, but Acheson wasn't paying any attention to anybody here in the room. His eyes were focused on something out the front window.

"Kid, why didn't you say something?" he demanded, turning to look at Duff now, everyone else forgotten.

"What?" Duff demanded angrily.

Fireman. Day One. Dumbass kid who can be trusted to make tea and cook burgers.

Barely.

"That?" Acheson pointed.

His voice had a fire to it now. Hard and ugly like a foreman about to tear a strip of hide off your ass for something. One hand pointed out the front windows.

Duff looked. He'd been paying attention to the rails and the far horizon down the line.

Something new had crept over the ridge above them on the right, coming over Sequoia and starting to build up steam as it rumbled down that last ridge like an avalanche.

Duff recognized it now, but he also knew how fast those things moved. It might not have even been visible when the pretty girl with the guns appeared.

"What?" the mastermind demanded. Like he really had better things to do with his time that listen to the amateur comedy routine Duff and Acheson had worked up.

"Storm coming," Duff muttered. "Big one."

He'd been out in the desert a few times when they came. Sandstorm like the old stories, but this was the biggest one he could remember. At least fifty kilometers across, horizon to horizon, and ten tall, a black wall of sand and ugliness.

Duff could see lightning arcing inside that cloud now. Bad news.

He wondered if the train was heavy enough to handle it.

"Not a storm," Acheson corrected him, voice and face both gone deathly white.

"No?" somebody asked.

"That's the Scour itself. Come for our souls."

CHAPTER 12

Red was in the corner watching all the emotions flow around the room. The old man engineer in a state of impending panic. The younger crewman who wasn't young, still driving but turned to his boss for directions because he was confused. Lefty standing there with both guns ready to just kill everything that moved while she laughed.

Matthias suddenly seemed at a loss for the first time since Red had known him, as his plan apparently didn't take into account something like a Scour.

As if any plan could.

Nobody knew where they came from or what spawned them. According to the oldest records, it was only a few hundred miles from here to the coast of an ocean that went on almost forever, so she had no idea if it carried with it all that sand and material, or just picked it up on the first land it touched.

But she knew what a Scour was. Everyone did.

Electrical storm that came across the ground like a blanket, ripping and tearing and shocking and shorting everything metal it touched. The mountain cities had been dug deep just to protect people against the Scour. The domes overhead didn't conduct electricity, so the SkyFolk were safe, and could even stand out on top of the plateaus and watch from nearly inside the storm.

Red had never done that, but she'd seem recordings someone had taken.

They were still pitiful compared to this beast.

"We gotta stop the train," the old man snapped at Matthias. "Lock the brakes and deploy the emergency anchors. That or we're doomed."

Matthias dithered. The young man driving watched Lefty.

"Do you understand?" the old man continued. "We will die."

"Fine," Matthias finally said. "Do it."

Red realized that she was leaning against a jumpseat that could be pulled down to sit, so she did. At this point, she didn't have anything she needed to do, and no experience with what was coming. Might as well be comfortable.

Lefty glanced at movement, but nodded at her an instant later, like she understood the need. Maybe she did. Red had no idea what really went on in that woman's head. She didn't think Lefty did either, at least half the time.

"Lady, please don't shoot me, okay?" the old man said as he sat.

Red grinned to herself as Lefty nodded. Everyone but Pedro had guns out right now, but the old man was treating Lefty like the only dangerous one here. Not the dumbest move on his part.

Red holstered her gun and hooked the little lanyard that would keep it in place. If she needed to be shooting in here right now, they were all already doomed.

The old man turned to his assistant.

"Duff, let go of the deadman and snap it hard back against the rear rest," he said. "That will set the emergency brakes on the wheels. Everyone hold on to something."

Red found that the seat had a belt like the men did, so she hooked it, just in case.

Just in time, too. The man in front of her pulled his arm back suddenly and the hum of the engine, that background noise just below the clack of the wheels themselves, vanished.

In its place, a squeal of metal on metal.

Red realized that the tracks they rode on were iron, and the wheels as well.

How did they keep from inducing a charge?

She made a note to look that up at some point. She doubted either of the railroaders would be interested in her idle curiosity right this moment.

The whole train jarred as the brakes suddenly went from pushing to madly digging in. Red was glad she'd buckled herself in, because everyone else suddenly was thrown forward.

She heard a gunshot ring out above the sound of the iron screaming for mercy. Red reached down and grabbed for her pistol as everyone staggered around, but she couldn't see anything.

No other shots followed, but she had her gun up, pointed at something, she wasn't sure. Too many bodies in the way.

"Damn you to hell," Matthias screamed in a rage so intense that you could have made a mountain out of it and dug your own city underneath. "What in the devil's name were you thinking?"

"I thought he was reaching for a gun," Red thought she heard someone else say back, but she couldn't tell and the noise was a physical pain.

She looked around and realized that the old man engineer

had fallen to the deck of the car. Blood was pooling beneath him and a good chunk of his head was missing.

The screaming stopped. Motion stopped.

Red wasn't quite sure if breathing stopped as well. Gunpowder smoke added a haze to the room and an acrid, acidic taste to the air.

Nobody moved.

"What happened?" she finally asked.

"This stupid shit just shot the engineer," Matthias snarled, ripping the gun out of Lonagan's hand and stuffing it into a pocket as the bigger man cringed away, like a dog expecting a kick.

Everyone turned to the other engineer. Red finally got a good look at the man.

Forty, give or take. He felt tall from what she could see. Broad across the shoulders. Tanned skin almost as dark as Pedro's but more golden, like you got from the sun, rather than your parents. Short-cut brown hair starting to gray along the sides.

He turned to Lefty and she caught his profile. The man had rough-hewn features, like a sculptor had found the essence of the man in the stone, but never finished polishing him down for beauty.

"Now what?" he asked her, like they were the only two people in the room. Maybe left on the Earth.

"The old man said something about emergency anchors before this moron killed him," Matthias yelled angrily. "Do that."

The man paused. Red could see various thoughts in his mind from the way his jaw muscles clenched. Measuring himself for a coffin, a long-ago boyfriend might have said about that face.

"I don't know how," he finally admitted.

"What?" Matthias screamed. "How is that possible?"

Again, a pause. Hard brown eyes stopped staring at Lefty long enough to glance at Matthias, but returned immediately. He knew who the most dangerous person in here was.

"This is literally my first day as a fireman," the man said slowly. "So far, I've learned how to make the train go, make it stop, and cook meals for Acheson."

"Who?" Matthias snarled, stomping a step closer but never getting in Lefty's way.

At least the man was still buckled in, so he couldn't surge up.

Lefty would kill him dead if he did. The man's eyes knew that.

"The man you just killed," the engineer said in a calm voice, pointing with only his hand, and not even his forearm. "Acheson Innes. Railroad Engineer."

"What the hell are you, then?" Matthias demanded.

"Two months ago, I was a lineman," the engineer replied. "Today, I became a fireman, because the kid who was supposed to have this shift called out and I got brought in at the last minute as a replacement."

Red wanted to watch the conversation, but the sky outside the front windows suddenly went black as a city tunnel when the power failed and only the battery-powered emergency lights showed you anything.

In here, two light strips came on overhead, dimly blue, probably on sensors that thought that night had fallen, or maybe the train had entered a tunnel.

It had, but this one was of a different kind.

She could hear the wind rising, screaming like a bevy of wronged women in a prison block at night, when the guards had locked all the newcomers down in their own wing and left them to understand what *years' incarceration* was going to feel like.

That moment when you could still scream, before you adjusted to living in a cell, maybe forever.

Outside, all the women who had ever died in that prison were howling at the train. Pelting it now with angry hands as they passed.

Red actually felt the springs underneath this massive car bow as the winds began to bite.

"Do something," Matthias demanded.

"If I move, she'll kill me," the engineer, the fireman, the rookie said.

Lefty surprised the hell out of Red by holstering both pistols without a word.

Just like that.

Even crazy women understood the old adage about fools fighting in a burning house.

Red had never been in a house that could burn. Her whole life had been in stone chambers and corridors carved out of living earth, except for three trips on a passenger train somewhere, when someone needed a safecracker's help to get at something.

The man let go a hard breath. Red did the same, obviously worried that someone might make another mistake and kill the one man who might be able to save them.

Outside, the Scour continued to grow, a false night falling.

CHAPTER 13

Duff took a deep breath.

Acheson was dead, two meters away. The smell of blood and shit was suddenly everywhere.

"Can someone wrap him up in a blanket and put him in his cabin?" Duff asked, hoping that it would improve things if people were in motion.

Mastermind nodded to the two men. They took off to the rear like the Scour had gotten inside the cabin already and wanted their souls.

Gunslinger just watched, moving around so that she was in his peripheral vision as she stood right behind Acheson's seat. Probably a subtle reminder on her part.

The whole car rattled and shook now. Duff looked out the front and day had turned to night in the course of about a minute.

He'd never seen a storm this big or moving this fast, but he was also further south than he'd ever been before, down where the craziness had more space to play, according to the elders who had taught him how to be a lineman.

He turned to the controls that Acheson hadn't taught him how to use yet. Ever.

Deadman switch made perfect sense. Forward for go. Back for stop. There was an extra back that he'd discovered when he pulled hard enough. That was the emergency stop.

Okay, so far, so good.

Speed indicator. Currently zero.

Elevation indicator. Currently going completely insane as the outside pressure dropped. Thing thought they were already at three thousand meters and rising fast, like the train itself was flying.

Temperature gauge. Inside a comfy twenty-five degrees.

Outside.

That can't be right. Forty-eight and rising? Shit. How hot did it get in the middle of a big Scour?

There were a whole series of buttons to push and little knobs he could pull out, but they were marked with cryptic letters, rather than words.

Like maybe he was supposed to be reading about his new job and taking tests next week on what all those things meant?

He turned to mastermind and shrugged.

"I got no clue," he said honestly.

The man screamed inarticulately. Pure rage or something. At least he had already holstered his gun as well, so nobody was pointing a weapon at him right now.

Most people would get nervous at that point. The few times it had happened to Duff, he'd seen red. Like now, but he was calming back down to human with every heartbeat.

"Look, I'm just a fireman," Duff snarled back at the man, willing to take it out on that guy.

Not the woman who looked like she'd just draw and shoot his eyes out.

"I can try crap at random, but that's about it," he continued.

The car rocked hard. Everyone staggered a step.

The winds howled so loudly that Duff would have to yell over them.

Duff had no idea how many tons the damned train weighed, but it apparently wasn't enough.

The two men showed up again, with a blanket. Acheson got treated better as a corpse than he had as a person, so maybe those two weren't as crazy as these three. They lifted him up and wrapped him in a burial shroud, each taking an end to carry the engineer aft.

The earth moved.

No, the ground was solid. *Postmaster Seventeen* just wasn't on it anymore.

With a lurch, the car became airborne, maybe the whole train, since Duff didn't hear anything breaking loose where those big buckles hooked the cars together.

That frightened him even more than just dying under these winds. It was like that ancient story where the tornado carried the girl away to another land.

Across the car from him, the wicked witch of the west suddenly had panic on her face. She almost looked human when she did that.

Duff screamed. At least he thought he did. Felt like it, but he couldn't hear over the shrieks of the Scour. Gunslinger looked to be yelling as well. Her mouth was open.

Emergency lights suddenly failed. Exploded, maybe, was a better term, as they threw an arc of sparks and fire across both side windows.

Everything dropped into slow motion as Duff watched.

The engine hit ground again. Only the left-hand wheels,

those right under his butt, from the feel. *Postmaster Seventeen* started to roll onto its side.

They'd been on a hillside earlier, cruising happily along the right-hand set of rails, but Duff got the feeling that they'd already been blown clear across the left-hand set.

A moment later, they started tumbling down the slope.

Gunslinger was thrown across the car at him, except that she was falling straight down and he happened to be under her when she did.

Duff grabbed her automatically as she slammed into his side, pulling the woman more or less into his lap with both hands.

Hopefully, the straps holding him in would be strong enough to keep both of them in place. Assuming the seat itself was bolted down tight enough for what was coming next.

She struggled against him.

He felt a hand go for a pistol.

"Hold still, damn you," he screamed into her face from close enough to maybe kiss her. If he really wanted to die. "We're not done rolling."

The Scour agreed. *Postmaster Seventeen* turned another ninety degrees with a lurch. Then ninety more, and Duff was hanging in the air with this woman in his lap.

She finally understood and wrapped her arms around his neck. It kept her from slipping out of his grip now and falling again, even as the train tumbled another facing, like an enormous dice in a craps game being played by the gods.

Or the devils.

Metal tore.

Duff felt it in his legs and butt, but the chair held. Maybe the five cars behind them breaking loose. None of them would weigh as much as the engine, being mostly empty space.

How far could a Scour carry an engine before it finally let go? How far would cargo cars fly in this wind?

Down.

Over.

Up.

Screams.

Crunches.

More screams.

Down.

Up.

Postmaster Seventeen took a wobble now, starting to tumble end over end in addition to flipping on its side.

Duff felt his head slam against the side window hard enough that he'd probably be seeing stars for a while, but his grip never slacked, even as he felt the woman in his lap screaming.

There was no sound.

Or rather, there was nothing but the sound of the Scour, a giant cat playing games with a mouse it had found in a cupboard, batting it this way and that.

Over.

Up.

Sky.

Ground.

Impact.

CHAPTER 14

Lefty came back from someplace far away.

Her ribs hurt. Her head hurt. Her wrists hurt.

Even her soul, if she really had one.

She was inside the cab of the train, wrapped snugly in Matthias's warm arms.

She opened her eyes.

It wasn't Matthias.

The engineer.

She remembered.

The memory was like a vid that she had watched years ago, rather than something she'd just lived through.

Falling off a mountain to slam into the earth below, like an angel stripped of her wings.

Falling from the heavens, to be caught by a fiend from the pit just shy of the flames.

Protected. Sheltered.

Safe.

Silence.

She remembered sound.

Something so solid she thought she might drown in it. Trapped in acrylic like a curio on some businessman's desk.

Lefty shook her head to try and get the cobwebs out.

The engineer stirred.

Even unconscious he had held on to her.

The train was laying on its side. She was on her back.

Lefty could see daylight fading through a gap in the far wall.

Sand and dust filling the air.

The man's eyes opened.

Lefty turned to him, almost bumping noses.

"Are you okay?" he asked, before he even looked around.

Lefty decided that she liked this man. Matthias had never thought of anybody else first, seeing everyone around him as tools and game pieces to be moved around. Things for him to use, abuse, and then fall asleep next to.

"I hurt," she answered him. "But we're alive, I think."

"Can you stand?" he asked. "I need to see what happened."

Lefty pivoted a little and slid off his lap. She stood on what had been the left-side of the train car, now down.

She stepped back as the man undid his harness slowly, falling a few decimeters to land on the hull when he finally got everything unhooked.

He rose slowly, gingerly, not getting too close in spite of the intimacy that had shared.

Matthias lay not far away. From the way his head hung in a different directions from the rest of his body, he'd been broken like a ragdoll.

Like she would have been, except for this engineer holding on to her as she fell from heaven.

Except that maybe she had been thrown bodily out of hell

instead. Lefty didn't think a heaven like the holy rollers talked about would welcome a woman like her with open arms.

Red moaned.

Lefty and the man both staggered over to where she had been saved by the harness she had slipped into when everyone else was just standing around pretending to be tough.

There was no sign of that idiot Lonagan, or the puppy Pedro. Lefty would at least miss the latter a little. He'd been good at what he did. And quiet the rest of the time.

Red looked a little worse for the wear.

Lefty stood to one side as the man knelt and peeled open one of her eyes.

She awoke with a start and thrashed out, but he caught both of her wrists carefully and held them.

"It's all right," he murmured to Red. "You're safe."

Lefty wasn't sure about that, but she wasn't about to argue the point.

Red looked a little muddled, but sucked a loud breath deep into her lungs and some of her fire came back to the surface with it.

"Ow," she said in a tiny voice.

"I agree," the man said. "Is it okay if I unhook you from the seat?"

Quiet. Calm. Like either of them might shoot him right now, which was an assumption Lefty could see anybody making, considering what had happened earlier.

Red nodded.

Lefty watched the man hold her with a hand underneath as he awkwardly unhooked things until Red more or less rolled into his arms.

He stood up and lifted her shoulders when he did. Red was tiny, even among women, while Lefty was tall.

The stranger had half a head on her.

"You got a name?" Lefty asked the man.

He turned to her warily, one arm still loosely around Red's shoulders as she was a little wobbly. She doubled over with a yelp, clutching her torso.

"Where does it hurt?" the man knelt, forgetting about her for a moment as Red got his attention and concern.

She decided maybe he was a good man, too.

"Ribs," Red gasped painfully, fighting to draw a breath.

"I'm going to touch you, miss," the man said. "It's probably going to hurt. I'm sorry."

He did something, and Red screamed almost as bad as the storm had been.

She collapsed, but the man caught her and sat her the rest of the way down.

"Pretty sure you've cracked a rib or two," the man said.

He turned to look up at her now.

"My name's Duff," he said simply. "There should be a medkit under the console between the two seats. Could you get it for me?"

Lefty thought about it and nodded, staggering a little as she had to walk in what had been the side of the cab when it rolled upright.

White box, marked with a big, red crescent on the edges and front.

Lefty detached it and carried the little briefcase back to where Duff sat next to Red.

"The best I can do it tape your ribs, miss," Duff was saying. "And give you something for the pain. Nothing feels broken, so it will heal pretty quick. Can I take your jacket off?"

Lefty was amazed, but figured the man must have had some medical training at some point. If he'd been a lineman, they had to be self-sufficient, being out in the desert itself for days on end, without a proper doctor on hand.

Red whimpered as he got her jacket off.

"Uhm, corset next," he said. "This is really going to hurt, but I'm going to have to squeeze you together some, and the bones are going to grind."

"Do it," Red hissed, crying now from the pain.

"Can I help?" Lefty surprised herself by asking, but the Ice Princess was in real pain, and Duff was trying to do right by her, in spite of them robbing his train and killing his boss.

Not the day Lefty had planned, either.

Duff looked up at her. Studied her now like he had in that first instant when her guns were between them.

"Hold her hands when I do this," he said simply.

Lefty knelt and took both of Red's in hers.

The first latch came apart easy enough. The second one caused Red to scream again and seemingly pass out.

Duff got the others done while she wasn't with them.

Red had a smallish chest under that corset, striped where the seams had pressed tightly into her flesh. Duff ran a hand down her side in a way that would have had Lefty squirming with ticklishness.

"Corset probably saved her life," he said under his breath.

"How?" Lefty asked, curiosity getting the better of her tongue.

He started and looked at her in surprise, like he had forgotten she was there.

"It held everything in place when she slammed into the side of the car," he said. "Otherwise, it might have driven a broken-off rib into her lung. We'd be watching her choke to death on her own blood right now if that had happened."

"Oh."

Lefty didn't really have a lot to say to that.

She might have been left alone with the man, wherever they were. At least she had Red still.

Lefty wasn't sure she really missed the other three men, which was a hard and cruel thing to say, but nobody had ever accused her of being soft and friendly.

Outside of bed, anyway.

Duff opened the kit and pulled out a roll of gauze tape and a small spray bottle.

He spritzed Red's side liberally and put the bottle away.

"I need your help," he turned to her now. "It would be easier if I held her upright and you wrapped her chest."

He touched Red a few centimeters beneath her left breast and on the hip.

"Start here," he continued. "Twice around, even with her belt, and then up some, but stay below her breasts. Then we'll hook her back into the corset hopefully before she wakes up again."

Lefty noted that Red's color was pale, but her chest rose and fell regularly. She grabbed the tape, found and end, and figured out how to get it around the smaller woman.

At least she had more experience with corsets than Duff did, so she was able to hook it easily as he laid her carefully down.

"Should I loosen the laces in back?" Lefty asked.

She liked the way he stopped and thought about it for a long moment before he answered. Matthias had never actually listened to her.

"No," he decided. "They'll help immobilize her ribs for now. Later, when she wants to sleep, we can, but I'd prefer if she kept it on for a couple of days. That will help immensely."

"Then what?" Lefty asked.

"Then we figure out where the hell we are, and how to get to safety," he said. "Unless you folks had planned to die out here in this desert."

CHAPTER 15

Duff wasn't sure if the black-haired woman with the pistols was still planning to kill him, but she at least looked a little more human now.

She rose and took a step back, studying him, but she wasn't reaching for her guns. Wasn't much he could have done if she did except die, even if he had been wearing his own revolver.

Never seen someone move so fast with pistols, even putting them away.

"You got a name?" he asked her, watching the smaller woman out of the corner of his eye. "Either of you?"

"She's Red," the woman said. "They call me Lefty."

"Lefty," he echoed numbly.

Sure, why not?

"And no, I hadn't planned on dying out here," Lefty said. "But Matthias was the one with the plan."

She gestured at mastermind. Duff had looked at the guy once and ignored him. He was long since dead by now. Lefty probably would have been too, if he'd been any weaker. Maybe Red would have been the only one who survived this mess with him.

Whatever the hell they'd gotten him into.

Red was more or less awake, but not moving much.

"Be right back," he told the woman on the floor. "My name's Duff and we've taped your ribs, but they're going to hurt soon. Let me know when they do. I've got some pills you can take then, but I need you coherent right now. Okay?"

Red nodded. Duff rose.

"Don't suppose this guy had anything on him that might tell us what he had planned?" Duff asked Lefty.

She shrugged and turned away from him completely, walking towards mastermind and kneeling at his side.

Duff took a couple of steps, but didn't crowd her. Still a dangerous, deadly woman. Hell, both of them had holsters with pistols right now. Duff didn't even know if the car with his gear had survived.

He glanced at the cracks and gaps where a side window had once been and noted that the sun was about to go down.

Acheson had mentioned waving at *Postmaster Four* as they went by. Something about late afternoon this time of year, but Duff assumed that they had missed it.

He also wondered if the Scour had picked up the other train and treated it as rudely as it had Seventeen.

Would they notice a missing train, if they had been far enough away to avoid the storm? Or assume that Acheson had gotten the emergency anchors deployed somehow and survived?

What the hell was the protocol in an emergency when someone stole a train right off the tracks, anyway?

Fireman. Day One. Dumb-ass kid.

The woman had been rifling around in mastermind's pockets. She pulled out a couple of pieces of paper now and studied one of them closely.

"Duff, you got a real name?" she asked in a sideways kind of voice.

Those menacing green eyes were back, pinning him to a wall or something.

Even kneeling, she'd shoot him dead if she wanted to right now, but he had no idea why.

"Torcuil Dubhthaigh," he replied evenly. "It's Irish. Duff for short."

She glanced down at the paper in front of him and rose suddenly. They weren't close enough to dance, but closer than gunslingers in a clearing, like they did in the vids.

She turned the paper toward him and Duff saw his picture printed in black and white, with his name across the bottom.

"Did you know Matthias?" she asked.

"Never seen him before," Duff replied. "At least as far as I know. Why the hell does he have my picture? Did?"

"Don't know," Lefty said.

She thought about it for a moment and those eyes got less menacing. Maybe.

"He did mention something at one point about having to kill someone," Lefty said off-handed. "The whole job was just a setup, sort of thing. You got an ex-wife that wants you dead, Duff Dubhthaigh?"

"Never had a wife," Duff replied, very carefully not moving due to the look on her face.

Cold. Calculating.

Deadly.

"Anybody else that might pay someone to kill you?" she asked.

It felt like a throwaway line on her part, but neither of them were fooled. She was talking about the mastermind who lay dead and broken at her feet.

And she was the one with the guns.

Something must have shown in his face.

"Who?" she asked, turning now to face him squarely, when she had been at something of an angle before.

"It's a crazy theory," Duff began slowly.

"I am not the sanest girl in the world, Duff," she retorted. "And you saved my life and maybe Red's, too."

He glanced back and the smaller woman. She was awake, flat on her back, head turned to follow the conversation. No guns in anybody's hands, yet.

Yet.

"So six weeks ago I was a Senior Lineman," Duff explained. "Got crossways with my union. Maybe other folks, too."

"Six weeks?" she asked, interrupting.

"Yeah, why?" Duff asked.

"Six weeks ago, Matthias suddenly started talking about a new job," Lefty smiled harshly, looking inward. "One where we'd make so much money we could all retire. Go on."

"They pulled me off the line and suspended me for a while as someone investigated my complaints," Duff said. "Then abruptly they offered me a new job as a fireman."

"Why?"

"Union rules," Duff nodded. "They can't fire me without a grievance process, and all of the ugly, illegal things I'd been complaining about would have come out if they did that. We made a deal. They moved me over here. I stayed quiet and finished out three more years and got my twenty-five pension. Nobody talked. Nobody went to jail."

"Except maybe they decided to shut you up permanently?" She rattled that piece of paper again.

It was his picture there in black and white, taken for his new identity card when he needed to be a railroader. The kind of image that should only exist in his personnel file. Except that someone had made a copy and given it to a total stranger that just happened to be robbing this train?

Duff felt everything go cold.

How close had he been to dead? And had that other guy shot Acheson, thinking he was doing his boss a favor, and just got the wrong guy?

Shit.

But for the Scour? Seriously, that was what he had to pin his hopes and survival on? The worst Scour he'd ever heard of?

Hopefully, they didn't come in waves.

Again, nobody knew. In ancient times, there was no such thing a Scour. Just wind and rain.

The War of the Gods had changed everything.

"I got no idea, Lefty," Duff finally managed, stopping himself from squirreling inward only by force of will. "Right now, I'd like to survive. We're going to need to figure out where we are, and then how to get back to the rail, so we can make it to either Olanchas or Capazon."

"There's another option," she said with a wicked smile on her face suddenly.

Almost made her look human. Certainly made her beautiful when she did that.

"What?" he asked, wondering what else was possible.

"Brigadoon," she grinned.

"That place is a myth," Duff sputtered angrily. "A fairy tale parents tell their kids about a magical tenth city that survived the ancient times intact. Where all the technology still works and the Scour never touches. There is no such place."

"There is, Duff," Lefty said, growing sober and serious as she eyed him.

He almost preferred her deadly, compared to this look.

"How the hell would you know?" he demanded.

She answered by turning the bundle of papers over and showing him something else.

"Matthias had a map to it," she said simply.

CHAPTER 16

Lefty liked the way Duff's jaw dropped open and his eyes bulged.

Honest emotion. Something she didn't think Matthias was actually capable of exhibiting. Other than that moment of pure rage there at the end, right before the storm took them.

She'd seen the man angry enough to hurt people a few times, so she knew that he hadn't been faking that.

Duff was more like an open book. And not a bad one, either. Like in one of those desert fantasy romances she found occasionally, although she wasn't about to suggest that to the man.

Especially since she'd just met him.

Even if he'd already saved her life once. And maybe Red's, too, since Lefty had no medical training that would have told her what to do with cracked ribs.

"You're serious," Duff said in a quiet, awed voice that was just about as opposite that Matthias had ever spoken as she'd heard.

"We were supposed to steal all the gold in back and then stop the train at some point," Lefty replied. "Presumably, so we could get off and walk to this place on his map. We'd have had enough gold to buy our way in."

"Gold?" Duff asked.

Honest confusion in those brown eyes. Open book.

"Whole big box of it," she nodded and pointed at the rear of the train. "Well, there was. You suppose it's still there?"

He glanced over her shoulder and squinted at something.

"We've got about an hour until sunset," the big man said. "Probably worth looking, because all my supplies and gear were in the second car, along with food and water. Hell, even blankets, and it gets cold at night on the desert floor."

He turned and took a step before he stopped and turned back.

"I think you ladies should come with me for now," he said simply. "If we can find it, we'll camp in the crew car. Then figure out where we're at and where we're going in the morning. Is that okay?"

Lefty nodded. Matthias never asked. Just issued orders and expected everyone to jump.

This felt more like partners, doing equal work for equal shares of things. Hell, he'd asked Red before touching her to save her life.

Hopefully, all that gold had survived, because splitting it three ways was so much money she might have to have grandkids, just so they could grow up rich.

"Red, I'm going to just pick you up, rather than dragging on your ribs," Duff stepped close to the tiny safecracker with red hair starting to gray.

Red nodded and clenched up tight, groaning under her breath.

Duff surprised Lefty, and maybe Red, too, by putting his arms under her legs and back and standing straight up.

Stronger than he looked.

"Can you get the door, Lefty?" Duff asked.

She moved ahead of the other two, finding the latch and pushing. The door fell all the way open with a loud clang, and she scrambled over the frame to stand up outside.

Valley floor. They'd been up on the hillside earlier, but all she could see of it right now was a line across. Looked several kilometers away.

Just what had that Scour done to them?

Duff emerged a moment later, standing Red up onto her feet and then stepping out as well.

Red was moving like an old woman, but Lefty figured she must be in an incredible amount of pain, even with the spray.

"Shit," Duff said as he looked around.

He turned the other direction and repeated the word.

Lefty did the same and echoed him.

Five train cars. Maybe. Lefty was reminded of peanut shells left on the floor of some of the nastier bars she'd been in, where they absorbed spilled liquor and vomit in equal parts.

All the cars had been dumped and tumbled by the winds, stretched out to the far edge of this wide valley like a snake chopped into five pieces. Six with the engine.

"Thoughts?" she asked Duff.

If he'd been a lineman, he knew how to survive outdoors.

Lefty had only ever seen the sun through windows on trains, or two times she'd been up SkySide with Matthias on jobs. Never actually walked around outdoors.

She said a small prayer of thanks that Lonagan had shot the other guy instead.

Duff might actually be able to get her and Red back to civilization. Even jail was better than dead.

She watched Duff kneel down and look at her feet, and then Red's.

"Good," he said to himself standing.

"What?" Lefty practically demanded.

"Neither of you are wearing heels," Duff said. "Walking across sand and stone with boots like both of you have on won't be as bad. Don't feel like stripping corpses of their shoes unless I have to. Done it, just don't want to repeat that today. Even if I have to."

She felt her own mouth drop open now. Lefty had done the whole stylish look today, but worn the boots with the low, wide heel, capped with a soft tip so that she could move suddenly and silently. Red always wore sensible flats with a good tread.

Lefty looked at the sand around them. No, dirt and stone. The Scour had picked up all the sand and carried it away, pushing it up against anything solid like a snow drift she had seen in old pictures. All the train cars had sand piled up on the near sides.

Such was the power of the Scour to reshape the world.

She turned back to Duff.

"Have to?" she asked, feeling long-suppressed curiosity grow bold enough to be seen in daylight.

"Got just this gear for now," he said, brushing at his pants and light shirt. His boots looked like desert gear. "My stuff was in the crew car, if it survived. Otherwise, I'll have to strip whatever I can wear off the other guy. Just as soon not, unless I have to. We can bury him proper in the morning."

He started to walk, slowly. After a moment, Lefty realized that he was moving at a speed Red could match, hobbling along.

Matthias would have already left everyone else behind and angrily snapped his fingers back at them to catch up.

Lefty let him lead, falling in beside Red and back a few steps, just in case the woman needed help.

She wasn't an Ice Princess right now. Hurt kitten was more like.

And Duff apparently had better maternal instincts for that sort of thing than she did, but Lefty didn't let that dissuade her. Linemen were teams, working out in the desert together.

Not criminal gangs where it was frequently every hooligan for herself.

The closest car was a hundred meters away. The air was still hotter than Lefty could ever remember feeling. Sweat started emerging everywhere, soaking her inside all this gear, where it cooled her.

Water would be a problem out here. Hopefully, the tanks on the kitchen car were intact.

The lack of noise was astounding. She'd always assumed that insects and small animals would make noise out here, but perhaps nothing had survived the Scour, or they'd been driven so far underground, like humans, that they had to take some time to emerge again.

She remembered from some of her books mentions of giant flocks of birds filling the sky, but those were the sorts of things that happened before the Scour.

Had any birds survived wild? Humans had chickens and rich people frequently had songbirds in gilded cages, but that wasn't an image she wanted to dwell on, so Lefty let it go and concentrated on her footing.

And making sure her new friends were safe.

They were all a long ways from home.

CHAPTER 17

Duff walked in shock. Autopilot, as the ancient term went. One foot in front of the other, solving what was right in front of him and not worrying about tomorrow until it arrived.

Anything else might make him crazy.

The train was destroyed.

Gone.

Folks back home would never even bother trying to recover the pieces, because the Scour had carried it kilometers across the valley, tumbling and shedding parts everywhere. And that assumed that anyone bothered looking clear the hell over here when the train failed to arrive at Olanchas.

They'd have felt that storm pass over. Nobody could have missed it.

But he didn't even know where Olanchas was, relative to where they'd been when the storm hit. Or where it had carried them to.

South, somewhere.

Was it going to be smarter to start walking south for Capazon? North for Olanchas?

Or was he really crazy enough to try for that shadowy legend known as Brigadoon?

If nobody talked about it, but it existed, it must be an outlaw kind of place. Hadn't Lefty mentioned buying her way in with gold?

One foot in front of the other. Solve tomorrow tomorrow. Hell of a first day for a fireman.

The crew car was closest, although the others were strewn back in a haphazard line. Two and three were a little closer but farther to his left. Must have been heavier.

The dark spot clear at the base of the hillside in front of him might have been car four.

Not today's problem. Maybe not tomorrow's, either.

He glanced back, and both women were keeping up, but he was also trundling along slowly, so Red could keep up.

He'd slipped a bottle of pain killers into his pocket so he had them close. She'd need them to sleep.

And he'd have to head back and grab the medkit if they were truly going overland tomorrow.

Would it make more sense to just walk along the railbed and hope one of the trains coming saw them?

That might have been smart if he'd been driving along on level ground, but they'd been up a slope. Not a particularly bad one, but not something he wanted to try climbing with an injured woman in tow.

Red would never make it up there.

Tomorrow.

Tonight, get cover, food, and water. Gear, if he could. Fewer troubles. Lefty knew how to use her guns, so critters would be less of a threat.

The gods must have had a black joke at his expense, when they got closer. The crew car had landed on its wheels, perfectly upright, like a giant had carefully picked it up and then sat it down clear the hell over here.

Until he got close, and saw the connector that hooked it on to the engine was gone. Just like that. Nothing there but the door into the car itself.

How much power did it take to tear that much metal and plastic?

Enough to carry the damned thing through the air like a toy.

Duff shifted his steps to the right, so he could approach from the back end and see how intact it was.

The nearest next car was another three hundred meters downrange. The mess was spread over kilometers of the valley.

How the hell had they survived?

Obviously, the gods were having fun with them.

The ass end of the car was still intact, from what he could see. The thing that hooked the two cars was still here, but he could see where it still held on to the matching piece from the car behind it.

Duff approached and found the ladder that led up to the door. It was still closed, so maybe everything inside wasn't scattered everywhere and destroyed. It was a train, so everything had a place where it got hooked down during transit.

Was that up to a Scour?

Was anything?

Duff nodded at the ladies and climbed. The door was mostly closed, but Duff could see where something had cracked it, some sort of brushing blow that just missed staving in the whole rear of the car.

At least it opened. Maybe the women had unlocked it when they broke in, and nobody had bothered to lock it up again.

Gold, after all.

Inside looked like he'd left it, however many hours ago.

Felt like weeks.

Insane.

He wanted to check and see if Acheson's body was there, or the other two men, but he had bigger responsibilities right now.

He turned to the two women who had come along to rob his train and maybe kill him along the way.

What a way to spend an evening.

There wasn't going to be an easy way to get Red up here. Nothing that didn't hurt.

"You hold her shoulders," Lefty said suddenly. "I'll lift her butt."

Okay, sure.

Duff got down on his knees and braced his hip against the doorframe, hooking his knee for leverage. It was only three rungs, but they'd be like hell for the woman.

He could read the immense pain in her face as she studied the ladder and reached a tentative hand. Lefty got close behind her and squatted down.

It took a lot of moaning and three separate motions, but they got her into the car. Lefty joined a moment later, moving like a gazelle as he backed up and stood.

Duff turned and took a deep breath.

"You suppose they made it?" Red asked from where she'd sat in the breakfast nook.

"Gonna find out," Duff said.

"I'll come with you," Lefty announced, moving close enough that her arm brushed his hip.

He studied the woman, but saw no trace of the lethal moll gunslinger he'd seen earlier. Just a woman. Hard and proud.

Maybe not planning to kill him.

At least, not yet.

She'd need him to get her to safety somewhere, whether it was Capazon or Olanchas.

Or Brigadoon.

Then, all bets would probably be off.

CHAPTER 18

Lefty watched the wariness in the man's eyes.

She couldn't really blame him, since they'd shown up to rob his train. And Matthias might have had plans to kill him. At least that was what the picture suggested.

She followed him at a polite distance as he crossed the kitchen. The cabinets had clear fronts, and everything was jumbled about, but they also latched shut, and the stuff was a good, hardy plastic, rather than the antiques that were so fragile if you dropped them.

Duff moved to the sink and opened the tap. Water came out, so he shut it immediately but she could see his shoulders relax, coming down some.

The bathroom door had gotten shut at some point. They peeked in but it was still in good shape. Even better.

Not that she needed a shower, but there was one. Bad use of water, but maybe she could wet a towel and get herself clean later.

Duff paused with his hand on the handle to the engineer's cabin. It was closed.

There was a stretch of time.

"Should I do it?" she whispered.

"No," he shrugged and turned the handle. "I'm fine."

The room was empty.

Lefty felt her own shoulders come down, realizing she'd been expecting to find three dead men in here, one with his head blown off and two more tumbled and broken like Matthias had been. But they weren't here.

The books were, scattered all over the floor as the checked, and the mattress had slid askew, but nothing they couldn't fix.

"Where's your gear?" she asked innocently.

Duff still flinched under her words. Like maybe he had a gun in there and was looking forward to grabbing it. Whether for insurance or to use it on her wasn't clear.

She grabbed him by the arm and turned the bigger man to face her in spite of her lighter mass.

"Whatever Matthias had planned died with him, Duff," she told the man earnestly. "The Scour wiped it all away. Now it's just the three of us, and we need to find a way to safety. I got no plans to kill you, nor does Red. I will, however, make you rich if things work out. Can we start there?"

He studied her face. They were close in this hallway, and the man was an open book, so she got to watch the emotions play out. Fear. Loathing. Hope. Maybe even a little lust, which she took as a good sign. If he saw her as a hot babe, she could possibly distract him from whatever demons and depression might be settling in on the guy.

It had been a day.

"Serious?" he asked, breathlessly quiet.

"Red and I would be dead without you, Duff," she let her voice get a little more schoolmarm now. "Plain as that. I owe you my life. So does she. That's a debt we take serious."

He finally took a breath. His whole body seemed to unwind a little as she watched.

"Okay," the man murmured. "Got a revolver like yours and a matching rifle, if my room survived. Plus all my line gear. With that, we have a chance of getting somewhere safe."

"Lead on, MacDuff," she said, causing him to stutter-step and double-take. "Old literary reference."

"Oh."

He stepped past her into the hallway and faced the next door a little more relaxed.

They still had seen no hint of the two men, or the corpse. Had the Scour caught them between cars when it pulled everything apart? The men would be nothing in that wind.

Just gone. It would be like they never existed, except in her memories of those bozos.

The door opened under Duff's hand and Lefty heard the sigh of relief.

She leaned close and peeked over his shoulder. Two bunks. Two trunks that had slid partway out from under the bottom one. Mattresses and blankets everywhere, but the car had turned over at least one and rolled or skidded a distance, from the scratches and cracks in the roof and one exterior wall she'd seen.

Duff knelt and jammed things around until one of the trunks was loose and he put it back atop the bottom bunk mattress. He opened it and she saw a heavy bag inside, buttoned shut but bulging.

He undid the various hooks and flipped the top flap back, revealing crammed contents.

Duff reached a hand in and pulled out a revolver by the barrel. He surprised the hell out her by handing it up for her to grab.

Not as good as the ones she had, but serviceable. And a statement on his part, that he would give it to her while he rooted around inside for something else.

Clothing, from the looks of it. Heavier pants than even Matthias had been wearing. A vest that seemed to be nothing but armored plates. A folded up longcoat far more beat up than Matthias's. Even a hard hat with a bowl on top and a palm-wide brim around the entire outside, with cloth hanging from the back to keep the sun off your neck.

Desert gear.

Lineman.

Lefty let herself find the first hint of hope she'd had since Lonagan had shot the engineer by mistake, just as the storm was rising.

Duff stood and unlaced his boots.

"Could you give me a little privacy?" he asked in a small voice.

"Sure," Lefty grinned and winked at him, watching the man blush just the weeest bit.

She tossed the revolver onto the bed next to him and pulled the door shut at the look of surprise on Duff's face.

Aft, she found Red, breathing shallow but awake.

"How are you?" she asked.

"Hurt," Red moaned. "Better, though."

"Good news," Lefty smiled as she sat next to the Ice Princess, just not close enough to accidentally jar her or anything. "Duff found his gear. And we've got beds we can sleep in tonight, so you'll be in better shape tomorrow."

"Yay," Red said in a weak sarcasm that sounded closer to the woman she'd been yesterday.

Lefty looked around, remembering she was in the kitchen car.

"You want something to drink?" she asked.

"That would be good," Red said.

Lefty let herself be nice to someone for no other reason than it felt good and rose. The refrigerator was a mess when she looked inside. It still had power, but she had no idea how long the batteries would last, or if they were recharging somehow.

Everything was in shatterproof containers, sealed up tight, so she took a moment righting it all and finding a container that smelled like lemonade. It was cold and wet. That would help.

She poured two glasses and left an empty third on the counter for Duff when he emerged.

Red moved like she was broken, which she was, but managed a few swallows in between ragged breaths. Lefty hadn't realized how dry she was until she emptied the whole cup in one go.

Desert air. No humidity, unlike the cities, where there was lots of water. She'd need to drink to function.

She remembered that, but she'd forgotten.

Red had a little better color when she put the cup down.

They might yet make it.

Duff emerged from his bunk.

Lefty remembered to close her mouth before she caught any flies in it.

He'd been in badly-fitting pants and a loose shirt earlier, but now he was the recruiting poster image of a lineman. Tough. Rugged. Sober. Confident.

Sexy.

Heavy pants with armored plates. Matching vest. Revolver low on his thigh, strapped down just like hers were.

It was as if he had transformed into someone else, just by changing clothes.

What had he said? Fireman on his first day of a new job?

This was the man he was supposed to be, standing in front of her.

Lefty felt like seducing him just on general principle, but that might be rude at this point.

She settled for a low wolf-whistle that made him blush again.

"There's lemonade in the fridge," she said as he stepped into the kitchen area.

He paused and fixed himself a cup as she watched.

Yeah, this was what a lineman was supposed to look like.

He slid into the booth on her other side, squishing her in between him and Red. She kept her commentary on the topic to herself. Red was even more restrained on those sorts of things than Duff was. Part of the reason she was the Ice Princess.

"Sun will be down shortly," Duff began after taking a long sip of the lemonade. "We'll be safe in here tonight, and then we can figure out what we're doing tomorrow. We've got at least some water, enough food for a few days, and gear."

She settled for consuming the musk of desert, sweat, and hard work.

Lefty watched him dig a bottle of pills out of a pocket and pop the lid open. He extracted one and slid it across the table to Red.

"This will put you out pretty quickly after you take it," he said. "I've got the bunk room set up for you to sleep, so we'll rack you out there. Lefty can loosen up your corset strings, but I'd like you to sleep in it tonight to keep everything in place."

Red nodded and just sort of stared at the pill.

"I'm ready now," she said in a voice just above a whisper.

Duff nodded to the two of them.

"Figured as much," he said, sliding back out of the booth and standing. "Let's get you put to bed then."

Red swallowed the pill with the rest of her lemonade. Lefty helped as they got her into the room. It was cleaned up completely, with the trunks tucked back like she'd seen the space before.

She pulled Red's jacket off as carefully as she could, and then turned her around and untied the laces that would let her breathe freer as she slept.

Once Red was down on the bottom bunk, Duff pulled the blanket over the woman and stepped out of the room. Lefty waited just long enough to make sure Red was asleep as the sun set and darkness fell outside the windows.

She emerged to find Duff sitting back in the nook, all contemplative and stuff.

"Now what?" she asked, sliding in next to him.

Not too close. Friendly, but not all *that* friendly.

"Should have brought the medkit over with us, but I wasn't really processing earlier," he said absently. "It can probably wait for the morning. Same with the rest of the cars, since we'll need to open up a mail satchel for you to carry stuff. I'd grab a spare for Red, but she won't be able to carry anything for a week at least, and by then we'll either be rescued or dead our here."

"Where are we going?" she asked the man.

He flinched. Blinked. Stared at her like she had turned into someone else on him.

"Not too sure we have much choice," he said after a long, brooding moment. "Don't know how far it was back to Olanchas when the storm hit. Or how soon someone might come out to find us. Storms like that usually do a number on rail beds, and that one was a doozy, so a full rail team is probably going to have to head south from the city, checking lines and fixing anything before they dare send any trains along it. Possibly landslides as well, with that much wind tearing things up. No idea how long it will take them to clear the right of way for someone to come this far south. We were several hours at full speed, so hundreds of kilometers, maybe. I don't really know. Farther than we can walk. That leaves Brigadoon."

"But you'll take us there?" she asked anyway.

"I got no more wish to die out here than you do, Lefty," he said in a quiet, tired voice.

Like her, he had had a day.

"Matthias was certain of Brigadoon, Duff," she said, just as quietly. "We were all set to stop that train at a certain point, jump off, and send it on its way. And it wasn't that much farther. He'd said we were about ten minutes ahead of schedule, so ten or so minutes ride down the track from the point I ambushed you."

"Then what?" he asked.

That was the crux, wasn't it?

Everything had been in Matthias's head, like usual. He had never trusted anyone to know more than the dead minimum. To him, she'd just been a gunslinger that he slept with, rather than a partner he trusted with anything vital.

"Then hopefully we can follow the map," Lefty said.

"And you said the gold would buy your way in?" he asked carefully.

"That was my impression," she replied. "Nobody really knows much about the place, but he obviously had contacts of some sort."

"A month ago, and I'd have been willing to bet on us sitting here and surviving long enough for a line team to rescue us."

"But?" she pressed.

"But you folks had my picture," Duff turned to face her and she could see the tired in his eyes. "Pretty sure that I wasn't supposed to be the one that drove the train into the station at the next stop. That means someone back in Levin didn't want me alive, and actually sent people to kill me. How much gold was there?"

"A box big enough that one man couldn't carry it easily," Lefty said, gesturing with her hands. "Fifty kilos of gold coins in it."

"Fifty kilos," he mused. "That's what a man's life is worth. At least I wasn't cheap."

He smiled weakly and she returned it, still not leaning too close to the man, as much as she might want to in other circumstances.

"Plus, if we're off in Brigadoon, nobody can ever talk about the folks that hired Matthias to kill you," Lefty completed the thought.

"Not sure I'm safe going back to the Nine Cities, Lefty," Duff said. "You know?"

"I understand, Duff," she replied.

And she did.

Red had been broken out of jail for this job. Matthias would have likely had the Rail Union after his hide for killing one of their employees.

She had a price on her head in any number of places.

Only one sounded remotely safe, for either of them.

He sighed and slid out of the far side of the booth. Rising, he reached out and turned the door lock that Red had picked earlier.

She shot him an inquisitive look that had some level of impact, but he sighed and shook his head ever so slightly.

"I'm going to bed," he said simply, heading up towards the front of the car.

She watched him go and decided not to ask if he really wanted any company.

Lefty hadn't slept alone in a long time. Not since she had let Matthias charm her into his bed the first time. He hadn't been all that fulfilling, but just having someone she could reach out and touch in the middle of the night, not even waking him, had been enough, most times, to keep the nightmares at bay.

She rose as well, watching him set the lock on the front of the car as well before he moved into the cabin across from Red.

"Good night," she offered softly.

He paused and stared at her for a long second. Again, staring into her eyes, looking for something. Whatever it was, he didn't find it, because he went into the other cabin and closed the door.

Or maybe he did find it. She couldn't be sure without asking.

She considered any number of excuses to knock right now. Maybe she needed a book to read? Maybe she was cold and could he warm her? Something.

But he didn't trust her. Barely knew her, in spite of saving her life already. And Red's.

She moved into the other cabin and checked Red's breathing. Long and firm.

Lefty stripped down to just her underwear, piling up boots, pants, corset, shirt, and armored brassiere, with her bowler on top and gunbelt hung from a handy hook where she could get at it in a hurry.

She climbed up onto the top bunk and pulled the blanket

up to her nose, wondering if it would be warm enough like this, or if she needed to grab a spare out of the linen closet she'd looked in earlier.

Tomorrow was going to be a new beginning.

What the hell did she do with the rest of her life?

CHAPTER 19

Morning.

Duff had the seasons ground into his bones by now, so false dawn was like a light switch, bringing him up from a dead sound sleep to full wakefulness between heartbeats.

He took a long moment and tried to remember where he was. Nothing felt right.

The memory of the Scour brought it back.

All of it.

He swung himself out of Acheson's bed and put his boots on first, having slept fully clothed, just like he did in the desert. He pulled the pistol from under his pillow and checked the load. Six rounds, midnight black faces in the cylinder when he popped it out.

He rose and finished dressing: pistol, longcoat, helmet, gear bag.

It felt like that final exam he'd taken, when they put a dumb kid in charge of the team and had him issuing orders to men decades older than him, just to prove he was ready to stop being a gandy dancer and become a lineman.

But he didn't have any old salts out there, just watching

under hooded eyes. Any mistake he made today might get people killed and nobody would step in and stop him from doing something stupid.

He opened the door and stepped lightly out into the hallway, listening for noise from the cabin where they girls had gone to bed.

Nothing, but he refrained from opening the door to check.

Instead, he moved to the rear of the train and put his bag and helmet down on the bench. A quick check and the refrigerator was still working. He had no idea how, without the engine, so there must be batteries somewhere. He did a quick inventory of the food that might go bad, but there wasn't much. Enough that he could make them a hearty breakfast and use it all up.

Then they'd be into cans and sealed bags and dry goods.

Just like he was home.

Except that he wasn't. Couldn't be, possibly ever again.

Someone had paid the mastermind a bitch-load of money to kill a dumb-ass fireman on his first day at work.

Hopefully, the gold was still intact back there, wherever that car was. With it, Brigadoon. Without it, he'd head for the tracks and flip a coin when he got there, heading north or south on the toss.

And hoping he found someone before the desert ate them all.

He got to cracking the few eggs Acheson had somehow gotten hold of. And that had survived all this mess, but they'd been packed tight. A few vegetables. The rest of the vatburgers, chopped into small chunks. Even some cheese.

Protein and calories. Hopefully enough water, too, as he had no idea where they might find a place to get some. At least he had a clicker in his gear if they found any. And a strainer that could get out most of whatever might be in it.

Lefty emerged as he started making noise. She moved like a ghost, but he caught sight of her as soon as she emerged.

And blinked hard, since she wasn't wearing anything but panties, with a pistol in one hand.

"I heard noise," she offered as she recognized him at the stove, cooking.

She didn't even blink at being mostly nude.

Porcelain skin, without a single blemish, near as he could tell. Duff felt himself blush automatically.

It doubled as she smiled at him and kept approaching.

"What's for breakfast?" she asked from a bit too close.

Especially with nothing covering those breasts.

"Everything," he stammered. "We'll eat, then check the other cars, and then see if the gods like us."

"We've already survived the Scour, Duff," she replied, sobering some from the mischievous grin. "Keep that in mind."

"Will," he said. "You should get dressed."

"Need a quick shower with a wet rag." The grin was back.

"Hurry," he offered, turning the heat down so things cooked slower.

She vanished into the bathroom and closed the door.

He finished cooking the mess about the time she emerged. The water in the tanks would be cold after the long night. That was what he told himself as she turned to face him for a moment, grinned at his stare, and then walked proudly into her cabin.

Duff swallowed heavily and started making coffee.

Lefty and Red emerged a minute later. Lefty was far less

distracting when she was wearing clothes. Okay, maybe not that much. She still drew his eye longer than was polite.

Red was looking better, but not great. She'd be days recovering, depending how badly those ribs had cracked. At least he could split the pills into quarters pretty easy. That should take the edge off the pain. Half of one, in a woman that small, and it would still be like she was dead drunk.

Three plates out and a pan of stuff. It smelled like mornings on the line, where every lineman took turns cooking, unless you had someone with the gift and the desire.

Chicory for everyone to drink, with some of the agave to cut the bitterness. Today, Duff missed the magical coffee they supposedly used to grow far in the far south. Something to perk him up for a while would have been nice.

Or course, those lands to the south were so hot as to uninhabitable now, at least as far as anyone knew.

They ate in relative silence. The sun was just coming up now, and it would quickly transition from bitter cold to sweltering heat.

Yet another reason why traveling would be so difficult. Duff was inured to such hardships, but both women looked much softer.

Stubborn as hell, so he figured they had the will, but you still had to have the body to cover any distance in heat or cold.

"Lefty, could you lace me up?" Red asked as she finished, last of the three from eating slow.

Duff moved to clean plates, then decided they could just be dirty. Water would be more important soon, and he didn't think he'd be back this way ever again.

One way or the other.

So he watched Lefty pull the laces with tender fingers, moving delicately as Red winced, stopping and starting again.

The face was the same cold killer that had stared at him over those barrels, but she looked different today. Not fragile. Duff doubted that she knew the meaning of the word, but maybe more delicate.

Like there was more to her than just a killer, and she'd decided to let others see that.

What had the mastermind been like? He'd felt like an asshole, but Duff had only known him for a brief time before the Scour killed the man and saved the women.

Duff didn't feel like he was a trade up, but who was he to say?

"Now what?" Red asked him, looking around and possibly seeing all this for the first time.

She'd most likely been numb with pain yesterday, but was just hurting today. He pulled out the pill bottle and spilled some into his hand, picking out the quarters he had chopped earlier when he made breakfast.

"Lefty and I are going to go check the other cars," Duff said, looking at the woman long enough for her to realize she needed to nod back to him. "Depending on what we find will tell us where we're going. A quarter of one of those pills should take enough of the edge off that you can move around and think, but not be completely intoxicated."

He watched the tiny woman take the pill with some of her coffee and sigh.

Nobody liked being immobilized with pain, but hopefully in an hour she'd be mobile.

"I'll just sit here then," Red said. "Not sleepy, and I can make it to the bathroom easy enough when I need to."

Duff looked at Lefty. Studied her. Remembered her with almost no clothing and blushed.

Interestingly, she blushed at the same time. He wondered if it was the same memory.

"You ready?" he asked.

"Let's do this," she replied, standing up right into his space and facing him squarely.

Duff resisted kissing her, even though he got the distinct impression she might not mind. Might even invite it.

Because she might yet be planning to kill him, no matter what promises she'd made.

Lefty followed the big man out the rear of the car into the morning sun. It promised to be hotter than anything she'd ever experienced before, just from looking across the wasteland before her.

"What's first?" she asked as Duff stopped and just pivoted in place slowly, apparently studying this entire valley.

For what, she wasn't sure.

"You need protection from the sun," he said, glancing at her. "Red as well. We'll grab your boss's jacket, and seen if Acheson had anything Red could use."

"Acheson?"

"The man you killed," Duff turned to her with harder eyes than earlier. "The engineer of *Postmaster Seventeen*."

"Oh," Lefty replied, feeling a little abashed.

She hadn't killed the man, but her people had.

She followed Duff to the engine, walking behind and to the side a step, rather than right up next to him.

Nothing had changed when they got there, but she wasn't sure what she had been expecting.

Matthias had started to smell at little, but they got his

jacket off of him, rifled his pockets for various things she kept, and carried the body out of the car. Duff pulled a folding shovel out of his big bag and dug into the dirt and stone while she watched.

Levering him in, Lefty said a quick prayer that maybe he would find what he was looking for in the next life, and not the hell that the holy rollers ranted on about, claiming that's where they were all headed.

Lefty wasn't sure they weren't already in hell, looking around the world, but you never won arguments with people like that, so it wasn't ever worth trying.

Duff had been nearly silent throughout all this, so when he looked up and spoke, she jumped a little.

"Gold, huh?" he asked out of the blue.

It took her a moment to understand.

"Oh, yeah," she said. "In that last car."

She turned and pointed. If the winds had carried everything in a more-or-less straight line, it was the one way the hell over there.

Damn, that had been one hell of a storm, hadn't it?

Duff put the digger away carefully and started towards the crew car instead.

"Let's check on Red," he said grimly.

Lefty fell into step, still back one and over one, where he couldn't see her blush.

She'd gotten so wrapped up in herself and Matthias she had forgotten to think about the other woman.

Needed to work on that. It was going to be more than just her against the world to get out of this. She had others now. And people who would be relying on her.

Red was fine when they got back, but that didn't change anything.

"Did they put the box back in the safe?" Lefty asked as they saw her. "I can't remember."

"Did not," Red said. "Going there next?"

"We are," Duff answered. "You okay?"

"Tired," Red replied. "But better. Staying here."

Her color looked good. More like what she'd been before.

Maybe they should spend a whole day here for her to heal?

"That's the plan," Duff murmured.

Lefty blushed some more, realizing she'd been talking to herself loud enough for the man to hear.

"We'll inventory today," Duff continued, as if she'd actually been talking, rather than just wool-gathering. "Get a bag. Maybe find some gold. Then start preparing food and water to walk across the desert. Not leave until tomorrow."

"What do we do if the gold's not there?" she asked.

"I don't know, Lefty," Duff grimaced. "Been thinking about that all night. Someone back in Levin apparently wanted me dead bad enough to hire you folks. Everything else might have changed, but that's still there, hanging over my head."

They fell into a companionable silence as they walked.

Duff led her to the closest car. It had suffered the worst, from what she could tell. Maybe it had been the one attached to the crew car and not broken loose clean?

It looked like some giant had grabbed it in both hands and twisted it. The metal bits underneath had held, but the plastic had peeled off and shattered everywhere, leaving a trail of black and gray pieces everywhere.

"Empty," Duff noted as they got close enough to look in through the broken side panel.

Sure enough, the Scour had tumbled it, breaking things open and sucking out all the mail bags that must have been there.

Just an empty shell now, like an egg that tunnel snakes had gotten to invisibly.

The next car was a little better off, if you could say that. Maybe the heaviest of the three, since it had stayed mostly on its side, plowing through the ground like a blade. She could see the path it had carved before the weight of the dirt in front of it was enough. The car was more like a mound that anything else.

But thankfully the end door was unlocked. They'd been in a hurry to get forward. Well, she had, and nobody had apparently thought to lock anything as they followed her.

Lefty shivered for a moment as Duff climbed in, realizing that they might have been in one of these cars when the Scour hit, but for being ahead of schedule.

Might have all been killed, except that the engineer, Acheson, had known about emergency anchors that they might have done something with.

Maybe that would have kept the train intact?

Matthias would still be alive right now. She'd still just be his moll.

But Lefty figured she could be glad the man was dead and not feel that much guilt about it. She'd never been that introspective, even though today felt like the dawn of a new her. A new lifetime.

Maybe she needed to become someone else?

Duff would, if the folks back in Levin were sending assassins. Bounty hunters would come next. And Lefty would have wanted posters up again.

Dare she just become Harper Solak and call it good? Nobody really knew her real name anymore.

Could they pull something like that off? Red had to have a real name, too. She'd need to get in on the act.

Duff stuck his head out and looked at her. Lefty flinched as his eyes met hers and he seemed to be listening to her internal commentary.

It was all still internal, right?

"You coming?" he finally asked.

Lefty nodded and climbed over the sill to join him inside.

Everything had just fallen over in here. It was piled neatly on the floor, or side wall. Whatever down was when it wasn't down.

Duff was squatted down, rifling through piles. He came up with a green bag that looked like an oversized purse, with a strap to go over the shoulder and the top flap turned down and closed with the cutest, little brass padlock.

The lock was no more than a statement of purpose, as fragile as it was. Duff agreed, because she watched him grunt once and pull out his pistol.

He wasn't going to shoot it off, was he?

No, the man just used the butt as a hammer. One blow. A second and the lock broke loose.

Duff smiled up at her. It felt right. There were all sort of laws about stealing mail. Especially from a mail train. Now, he was a criminal like her. Like Red, too.

Inside, he dumped out a bunch of envelopes and a few small boxes.

"Anything worth stealing?" she asked automatically.

"Be my guest," he replied, standing and moving towards another pile.

Lefty looked at the two little boxes. One was a cube. The second was wide and flat, like a jewelry box she'd had once for a special necklace she'd stolen. You laid it in there and closed the top down on a hinge.

It was taped securely shut, but reminded her too much of

that old necklace, so she slipped it back into the bag as she slipped the strap over a shoulder.

She could always open it later and see if was anything actually interesting, but for now, the mystery and the reminder was enough of a thrill.

"Don't see anything else," Duff said.

Lefty had to agree. She followed him out the back door and onward. The sun was climbing now, as was the temperature. They'd have to stay under cover during the day if it was already this hot this quickly. She could only imagine what noontime was going to be like.

Perhaps just for completeness sake, Duff hit the third car. It was in better shape that the first and worse than the second. Nothing inside looked remotely interesting, since Duff wasn't going to get Red a bag. Plus, she had her backpack. Pedro had taken it off when she sat down in the engine, and died leaving it to tumble around.

They could get it later, but she wasn't sure who would carry it.

Last car.

Lefty felt excitement take hold, warring with fear. All the cars had tumbled and broken, scattering pieces everywhere, those that weren't just carried away by the wind like the bodies of the three men.

The outside shell was covered with crazed tracks, but the egg itself seemed intact.

Dare she hope?

Lefty could see her future split right down the middle, the road of the rest of her life suddenly forking. One way, wealth. The other, back to one of the Nine Cities, starting over again without Matthias and his contacts and dreams to keep her going.

She didn't dream. Too much work. Lefty knew she would coast.

With enough gold, she could coast forever. And might.

Duff looked over at her.

"I'm giddy and nervous," he admitted.

"Me, too," she said, willing to open herself up that much.

He'd saved her life. And Red's. And then left them alone to sleep instead of putting any claim on her that she might not have necessarily resisted.

Same this morning, when she'd even teased him with her near-nudity, just to see what kind of a man he was.

Duff was a good man. Lefty wasn't sure she'd ever met such a magical creature in her life. And wasn't sure if she wanted to keep him around.

What would a life of honesty be like?

"Let's do this," she announced, stepping forward and pushing the door enough to look inside.

Lefty felt her heart start to hammer in her chest as she did.

The interior was dark. Gloomy.

That safe had broken loose from where it had been, or maybe never been bolted down, as it was perfectly upright, while the car was on its side.

She opened the door up against gravity and looked closer.

The box was there.

Lefty let go a sigh.

Duff was right beside her.

"That it?" he asked.

"It is," she breathed, watching Brigadoon unfold in front of her in all its glory and greed.

He did something and the door latched itself up in the air.

"After you," he smiled.

Lefty slipped in and found her footing easy. The car had

been empty, save for that safe and the box, Someone had latched the box shut again, because there weren't coins and rolls scattered hell and gone around the inside to be chased down.

Duff slipped into the darkness with her.

She turned and he was there. Too close, but she didn't back up.

He didn't either.

They both blushed at the same time and turned awkwardly to the interior.

Lefty could smell him. Matthias had worn a cologne at all times. Sickly sweet, compared to the honest sweat of a man like Duff. It overwhelmed the last traces on the Matthias's longcoat.

That was good.

They walked to the box, laying on its side.

Duff grunted and pulled it upright.

"Damn, that's heavy," he exclaimed.

"Gold," Lefty answered. "*Screw you money*, as my mom used to say when I was young."

He undid the latch as her heart began to pound again, certain that little fairies had snuck in and stolen everything. Replaced it with lead when nobody was looking. Maybe the car had been open to the Scour somehow and it had reached in and taken all her gold, filling the box up again with sand when it was done, just to tease her now?

Duff popped the top open and whistled. Lefty leaned over his shoulder, smelling him even sharper, to enjoy the look of all that wealth, just waiting for her.

"Okay, I have to admit it," he said as he pulled out one of the sleeves and opened it carefully, a coin dropping into his gloved hand. "I didn't really believe you."

"I'm not sure I believed me, Duff," she breathed heavily into his ear. "Wanna rob a train with me?"

He turned and suddenly was there. Kissable, but somehow distant.

She'd have to seduce him if she wanted that kiss, but she wasn't sure how right now. But the gold would help.

"Guess I'm a thief now," he said quietly. "Going to steal all sorts of things?"

"Maybe," she offered, almost touching noses with the man. "Got anything in mind?"

"The world just changed," Duff whispered. "New beginnings."

"Turn into completely different people," she nodded, agreeing. "Not who any of us were before."

He nodded, pensive.

That kiss was just dangling there, but she could see his reserve. And she wasn't sure how to cross whatever chasm was there to steal it from him, so she didn't move.

He didn't move, either, forward or backward.

She could see it in his eyes, an open book for her to read.

Fear.

Of her?

Oh.

Right.

Killer.

He remembered her as she was staring down those barrels at him. Saw her holding that picture of him that Matthias had. The contract for Duff's death, with all this gold as the payment for it.

"That was yesterday, Duff," she said quietly. "Today, I'll be whoever you want me to be. Whoever you need me to be."

He recoiled a little at her words. But not far. She could see understanding dawn in those eyes.

Becoming someone new.

They'd have to. The gold would just make it easier, but they'd be stealing a whole bunch of it from a mail train.

Those folks might send an angry posse after you for that sort of thing. Nobody would ever know the truth, except what the three of them told anyone.

"It will never be this easy again, will it?" he asked, like maybe he could read her just as easily.

No man ever had, but no man had ever really looked, as far as she could remember.

"Gold will make it easier," she offered, understanding the pain that was suddenly there in his eyes.

A man who had now lost everything twice. The career that was his dream. The thing that he had hoped to carve out from the remains.

Now, he was going to become a train robber.

Like her and Red.

He didn't kiss her, but she could see it in his eyes.

Desire.

She'd been lusted after. A body this great and killing skills turned many men on, but she had the feeling she could be sackcloth ugly and covered with grime and this man would still smile at her.

They would kiss tomorrow.

One of the tomorrows.

She could live with that.

They both nodded and rose, like they'd just spent hours working out the details. Maybe they had.

She was looking forward to talking it over with him.

Duff put the coin back and closed everything back up.

He grunted and staggered under the weight as he lifted the box.

"Let me help you," she offered.

"You get clear outside and I'll carry it over," he growled, teeth clenched. "We still got to get this back to Red and figure out what to do with it."

"We're not taking it with us?" she asked, shocked.

"Too heavy," he replied as they moved. "Need to take some and hide the rest."

Oh. Good. He was already thinking like a thief.

That would help.

Brigadoon was supposed to be a city of thieves.

Duff carried the stupid box over the sill and let it settle the last little bit onto the hard-packed soil outside. He was now officially a train robber, when you got down to it.

Literally, and not just in his mind.

Duff climbed out and studied the dangerous, beautiful woman standing there looking at him expectantly. He'd never been good with women. One of the reasons the line called him.

Easier to just stay out in the desert and not have to figure out what a woman might want. Most of the linemen and women were like that. Had a someone or two in town, but after all while, they got too rowdy to be settled down. Some husbands and wives understood that. Others didn't.

Duff had never looked close enough.

Until trouble came looking for him.

And she was. Twenty-four carat and hard as nails. Armed to the teeth and ready to kill.

And somehow soft, in ways he really didn't get. Like she'd pulled in all those sharp edges around him so he didn't end up bleeding, even accidentally.

Lefty watched him now, and Duff had the impression she

was hanging on his next words. Like maybe he had some grand wisdom he'd magically picked up on the rail at some point from one of the old farts who didn't know any better either.

He smiled at her instead. That much was honest.

She smiled back.

"Gimme a hand?" he asked.

"Sure," she slipped to one side and grabbed hold of the other handle as he let go.

Maybe she brushed up against him a little as she did. He couldn't tell if it was accidental.

They moved. He knew it would take a while, double so with this much weight. Start and walk for a while, then stop and rest.

Sun was a third of the way across the sky by the time they staggered close to the crew car and collapsed in the shade of the machine.

Red was standing on the back deck watching, but made no effort to help. That was good. Duff would have yelled at her if she had.

Better to spend days healing while food and water were available. He still had to study mastermind's map and see if he could match it to what he saw, based on what Lefty knew.

"It's really there?" Red asked, like maybe she hadn't believed it either.

"Really is, Red," Lefty called back.

Duff sucked a deep breath down and stood up again, grabbing both ends of the box and lurching enough to get it up onto the deck next to Red.

Lefty followed and they all ended up inside.

Wasn't all that cool, but at least the sun was blocked in here.

Red looked better, too, like maybe just sitting and meditating all morning had helped.

Duff had been doing a lot of thinking, but didn't have a lot he knew. He found himself somehow sitting tucked in between the two women in the booth when they got settled, glasses of cold juice from the refrigerator in front of them.

He wasn't sure how he felt about that symbolism.

"So we're rich," Lefty said with a broad grin that didn't look at all like the woman who had pointed guns at him yesterday.

Especially the *we* part.

"Sort of," Duff agreed and countered. "Do either of you know anything about this so-called Brigadoon?"

"Nothing," Red said. "Just heard the name in children's stories, and then when Matthias explained that he had an escape for us, but not how."

Lefty pulled the map from a pocket of mastermind's coat and unfolded it onto the table in front of them.

Rail line running down from the mountains. The valley was much wider here, spreading out as it made the long run down to the Angel Mountains that separated Capazon and Jacumba from the rest of the world up north.

Terrain got rougher as you headed east. The rail bed had mostly followed an ancient highway for foot traffic in the old times, but in a few places they had to shift. Earthquakes had changed things so much over the years, and still bounced things around with stunning regularity.

Part of why everyone needed lineman, fixing everything after ground shakes and scours tore it all up, so that civilization could keep going.

Duff had been studying the terrain this morning. Automatic habit, since you needed to know where slides would originate or where a fault might be buried and uncovered by a sudden quake.

They weren't that far from Atoll, which he assumed was a play on words, since it meant island in some language. They were way inland, even from where the waters had come up from the south and drowned so many places. There was an ancient lakebed farther south, but the old geezers had said that it was dry before there were even humans in the area, so Duff assumed no islands worth mentioning.

"We're here, I think," he announced in a careful, unsure voice, pointing to a spot south of the ruins the map had marked as *Red*, like the woman next to him.

Both women sidled up closer to him, almost in harmony. He held his breath and kept his elbows tight.

"Here's Brigadoon," Duff continued, shifting his finger. "At least according to this map. Straight line walk a little over twenty kilometers, but I assume terrain will get in the way and we'll end up walking closer to thirty to get there."

He paused and looked at each woman in turn. Both nodded.

It didn't help his state of mind that both were simply gorgeous in their own ways. And relying on him to save their lives.

And his own.

He shifted enough to point out the window that had survived the tumbling and crunching that had done so much damage elsewhere on the car.

"That mountain there sure looks like this one here," he tapped the map.

"So we can do this?" Lefty spoke up.

"We can try," Duff replied. "If I'm wrong, we're probably going to die out there."

"We're already dead, Duff," Lefty's voice got something. Not softer, but less hard. "That wind picks us up and breaks my neck like it did Matthias. Red, too. The boys are simply gone, sucked away and never to be seen again."

"I'd like to survive," Duff said.

Red surprised him by leaning her weight against this shoulder. Companionable, like.

"Me, too," she offered. "But we can't any of us go back to the Nine Cities. You know that."

Duff wasn't sure how much of everything she'd understood, but apparently enough.

Duff glanced down at her. The woman was all legs, so he was nearly a head taller seated. Same with Lefty.

Felt weird.

Even more so when Lefty did the same thing Red was doing, leaning against him.

What the hell?

But they were right. He'd saved both of their lives. And he had to keep doing that.

Duff sucked a breath clear to his toes and let it out again.

"So we have to figure out what to do with that gold," he began, feeling both women startle, since they were pressed against him now.

Both leaned back, again in a harmony that was weird, because he was pretty sure it was accidental.

Pretty sure.

"It's too heavy to carry thirty kilometers with all the rest of the stuff we have to bring," he continued.

"Leave it here?" Lefty gasped.

"Gods, no," Duff said. "Pretty sure some line team will show up eventually when we don't arrive. If we did, they'd get it. Not my preference."

"So what, then?" Red asked.

"We need to maybe get everything ready today so we can leave at false dawn tomorrow," Duff said. "Start walking, with some of the gold on our persons and the rest in that box. We'll carry it as far as we can, trying to get around the southern face of that mountain right there. That gives us afternoon shade, so maybe we can walk farther."

"Bury it?" Lefty realized first.

"Yeah," Duff agreed. "Find us a spot along the way where maybe nobody can see us, from either end, and then hide it. We'll take some with us, and then return later for the rest when we're healthier and have the right gear to carry that much gold around. Maybe even a wagon or something."

"Either end?" Red asked tentatively.

"I gotta figure that a city of outlaws that doesn't trade with the Nine Cities is gonna have somebody somewhere watching for stragglers coming in off the desert," Duff replied. "Especially if they were expecting you folks after a train robbery. Don't want them stealing the gold you ladies worked so hard to steal in the first place."

That got smiles from both of them. It felt good.

Because, damn it, if he was going to be a railroad thief now, he was right sure going to do a good job of it.

CHAPTER 22

Red watched the byplay between the man and Lefty. She could see the patterns emerging.

Lefty was a broken, hollow kind of person. Red knew that. Needed someone to direct her energies and give her purpose, otherwise Lefty would just sort of float through her days.

Matthias had filled that previously, giving Lefty a job she could do and dreams to go with them. But Matthias was dead, good riddance.

The fireman was going to take over that role now. Lefty would continue to be a follower, more or less, but Duff was the person giving orders.

Red didn't mind for now. Most of yesterday was a blur, but Lefty had explained a few things to her while they got ready this morning. Including the woman's opinion that Duff was a *good man*.

Whatever the hell that meant.

Today, she was all taped up and in far less pain. The first piece of pill was slowly wearing off, so she had a long nail being pushed into her side again, but she could think.

Duff was used to the desert as a former lineman. And had his own reasons not to go back to the Nine Cities. Nor to turn the two of them in for any reward, even if that meant that he couldn't keep the gold.

The plan to bury some of the gold was good, too. They could have enough to be wealthy, but not so much that they risked being attacked by someone when they got to Brigadoon, unless the place was even more of a lawless hellhole than she'd imagined.

Duff was staring at her.

"You're white, all of a sudden," he said.

"Pain," she replied, realizing that it had doubled in the last few seconds.

Duff checked his watch.

"A little early for the next one, but maybe you should take it and lay down," he said, digging out that bottle from his pocket. "Lefty and I can spend some time organizing things and fill you in around dinner."

Red nodded. The next bit of pill got swallowed and she stood up.

Too fast.

Everything got blurry and started to spin.

Red would have cracked her head on the table, but Duff was there, catching her before she wobbled too far and suddenly she was lifted up in his arms and carried back to the bunk.

Through the tears of pain, she tried to thank him. Maybe even tried to grab him for a kiss, but she wasn't sure.

Once he got her flat, the pain suddenly went way down, like maybe she'd been sitting wrong. Need to remember that. Maybe have Lefty sit on the floor to talk to her later, so she didn't have to move.

Red closed her eyes and concentrated on breathing shallowly. There was a lot that needed figuring, but she knew that the world would be sliding away from her soon.

Could they really trust this man with her life?

143

Lefty watched, fearful that Red was more seriously hurt than they had thought. Duff saved her though, and got her to bed while Lefty watched.

He might have two women making passes at him soon, from the way Red had acted as they all got there.

Lefty tried to decide if she was jealous. Or even if she should be.

Matthias had never been monogamous. She was just handiest, when the man had a need. Red had never so much as looked at Matthias, so Lefty had had the boss to herself when she wanted company.

Now, they both had Duff.

And he didn't look like he had the slightest clue how to handle that.

"You ever been married?" she asked him as they sat back down with their juice.

"Nope," Duff said. "Line work doesn't lend itself to that."

Lefty had no idea what that meant, but Duff seemed sure, so she tried a different track.

"So what would you do, without yesterday?" she continued.

He went deep and introspective in ways that left her a little confused.

Mostly, she also didn't do introspection. Too much risk of falling back into the dark places she had only barely managed to crawl out from the first time.

"I don't know," he said finally. "Been on the line since I was sixteen."

"How old are you, Duff?" Lefty suddenly wondered.

He was grizzled, but not worn out or used up. Aging like a fine wine, to hear her mother's ghost describe the man.

"Thirty-eight," he said, turning his gaze her direction now. "Been doing that work for twenty-two years. You?"

"Twenty-six," she admitted, feeling like a decade as a gunslinger was an eternity.

Duff nodded at whatever it was he saw in her eyes now.

"Red is thirty-one, I think," she continued. "Not sure, but I seem to remember a wanted poster with her face on it."

"If we're rich, I might become a man of leisure," he said. "Whatever the hell that means. Not like I got a lot of skills fit for regular people."

She could understand that. All she had was her guns. And her beauty, she supposed, but she'd never get that desperate.

Not while she had guns.

"Do you know anything about Brigadoon?" he asked.

Lefty tried to remember bits and pieces that Matthias had shared or muttered at various times.

"It was a city before, I think," she said. "Dug into a mountain like the others, but nobody lived there. Someone found it later and began expanding it, but the folks in charge then didn't like the SkyFolk of the Nine Cities, so when the railroad was built, Brigadoon got cut off. Supposed to have died as a result, with folks returning to the Nine Cities, but Matthias seemed to think that there was some trade in people and goods going on between the two sides."

"Makes sense," Duff agreed with her. "Folks vanish from the cities and show up later, usually saying they've been on one of the others, but they could just as easily have been at Brigadoon. Bad place?"

"Matthias described it as a den of thieves," Lefty nodded. "But mostly honest ones, if there is such a thing."

Duff shrugged.

"If gold is gold, then just one of those sleeves of coins is enough for each of us to live a life of luxury for a while," he said. "Assuming we survive, we can figure out how to get back for the rest."

"Would you ever go back to the Nine Cities?" she asked, suddenly nervous that he might do that.

Might just leave her and Red at Brigadoon. Red would be fine, but she was human.

Lefty wasn't sure what she was anymore.

She'd be hollowed out, a doll with nothing inside, sitting on a shelf.

At least she knew that much about herself.

"I don't think I can," he said gruffly. "Not unless I can turn myself into someone else."

"I've done that," Lefty said. "Nobody remembers Harper these days, I don't think. But if we had money, we could buy someone else's identities and live as them, instead."

"We?" he asked her now, those dark brown eyes locking onto hers in ways that reminded her of men she'd killed in gunfights.

Hard. Stubborn. Focused.

Interested.

She thought about her answer instead of just blurting it out in the heat of the moment.

It felt like a chasm had just opened up at her feet. Maybe an elevator door had opened up but the car wasn't there and she was about to fall to her death down the shaft.

"Yes," she decided. "Us. You. Me. Red if she wants to. You saved my life, Duff. You saved Red. You'll do that again if we make it to Brigadoon. That makes us a team, at least as long as you want such a thing."

She felt the pleading in her eyes, but couldn't speak it out loud, in spite of wanting to. Needing to.

Needing him.

Though if she was being honest, she really just needed someone.

However, Duff was the best person she'd ever met, as near as she could tell in a life of crime and murder.

He was an honest man.

Lefty wasn't sure how many of those she'd ever met.

At least the ones she wasn't in the process of robbing.

He sighed. It didn't sound like pain, but she wasn't sure. Plus her own heart was banging loud enough in her ears that the winds might pick up again and she'd miss them.

"You sure?" he asked, as if maybe he'd misheard her.

Lefty gasped a breath in when she finally realized she'd stopped breathing. Fought to keep her heart from exploding.

He looked like he was considering her offer.

Had it been an offer? She hoped so. Words had never been her thing. Not when guns spoke more eloquently in her hands.

"I'm sure, Duff," she said over the roaring in her ears.

"And after we get there?" he continued, voice dropping

lower and quieter enough that she had to lean close to follow him.

"I have no friends but you two," she admitted finally. "Nobody in the world that I care about, and that might care what happened to me. I've got to protect that."

He recoiled a little, like she'd slapped him, but she hadn't moved.

It was there in his eyes, though.

Loneliness.

Not just being alone, but not having anybody to talk to about it.

That was the thing she knew, especially when it snuck up on her at night and slipped into her bed to cuddle, like she was thirteen again and afraid to make a sound when her father came, or she'd be beaten some more.

Duff didn't have any of that in his eyes. She'd looked closely more than once. Did so now, just to make sure.

The only thing she saw in there was fear. Not of her, but of being alone.

She could understand that. It was there in the mirror every morning, before she put on her bravado and guns.

"Okay," he whispered, moving just enough to nod.

Lefty felt like screaming for joy. Or hugging the man. Maybe dragging him off to the other cabin to celebrate, but he looked too fragile.

She sat perfectly still, like he was a mouse that might spook at the slightest movement.

The moment stretched out. Finally, he remembered to breathe. She did the same.

"Where do we go from here?" she asked carefully, utterly at a loss for what he might need or want.

He blinked and seemed to come back to her from a great distance.

"We pack," he said quietly. "There are canteens and containers here we can fill with water. Food to pack. Coins that we need to pull out of the box and hide on our person and in our gear."

"How much?" she whispered.

"I think a sleeve each," he said, suddenly grinning ear to ear at her. "If we each have three or four coins in pouches, and hide the other six or seven, we'll be rich, assuming we can get there, get in, and convince a bunch of cutthroats and thieves to leave us in peace."

"I can definitely make any man understand *No*, Duff," she grinned back.

"Yes," he agreed with her. "It's the *Yes* part that makes me nervous."

"It will be good, when we get there," she assured him.

"Yeah," he said. "When we get there."

Afternoon. The sun had crossed the clear sky while Duff worked.

About a third of his gear had been pulled from his big bag as Lefty and Red watched silently, seated at the table with him. He wasn't going to be doing line work anymore, so there was no reason for it.

The mess kit stayed. The medkit got upgraded with a few things from the train's version. Spare barrels and a box of ammunition that fit both the pistol and the rifle. Compass. Clicker. The basics.

He no longer needed a spare surveyor's transom. That was just one he'd picked up along the way, and he was never going to have to measure rails and spacing again. Same with a lot of the other stuff. Heavy, bulky, or unnecessary.

Instead, the spare pants he'd worn. The socks. The hardhat stayed, but he strapped it to the outside, because he'd be wearing it as they got out into the desert.

Duff did tuck a spare coin into the lining of the hat, more as a good luck charm than anything, but linemen were as superstitious as anybody.

Neither of the women had spare clothing beyond what they had on, but Acheson's gear included shirts they could wear like tunics and pants they could adjust as needed.

Most of the bulk and weight was going to be water and food.

Gonna be hot and dry walking.

Thirty kilometers was nothing to cover when you were rumbling along in a lineman's car, but you were moving faster than that anyway. Here, he'd be on foot, with two women who'd both told him they'd never been out on the desert floor before.

They needed hats. Well, both had hats, but neither were appropriate for the desert, so he cut up one of Acheson's shirts to make something they could wear with their hats to protect their necks and faces from the sand.

There might also be stinging insects out there.

Lefty had spare barrels and ammunition as well, but not nearly as much as Duff did. Worse came to worst he'd give her his gun for one of hers. Red had nearly as much ammunition as he did, but her gun fired a smaller bullet, and was a single-shot you had to crack in the middle after every round.

They ate dinner in companionable silence, the weight of tomorrow on everybody's minds. Plus, Red was on edge from pain, and about to take a whole pill to help her sleep.

Lefty was practically vibrating with energy, but had remained pretty quiet all day, just asking the occasional question.

Red studied the two of them over dinner with humor in her eyes.

Didn't look like trouble, but Duff didn't understand women in the first place.

He'd just sat and listened as Lefty had explained everything to the other woman. The two of them looked like they'd have a conversation later, when he wasn't around. Maybe after they got to Brigadoon and figured out what they were going to do with the rest of their lives.

Red took her big pill and he and Lefty got her to bed and tucked in.

Duff returned to the kitchen and watched the sky outside turn dark, stars emerging.

He'd worried secretly if a line team might make it this far today, but nobody had.

He had no idea what that meant. Maybe they'd assumed that the train would somehow anchor itself to the ground during the storm and then come in late? If so, they would wait a day and set out tomorrow, presumably.

That would give him and women time.

He'd watched science fiction videos about the time before, when it was safe to fly in the air, rather than hugging the ground any time you have to be outdoors.

Duff could only imagine what it might be like to take a train that could fly over all the terrain, not having to slow down when going up or down, or watch for slides that might bury the line and cause you to derail.

Nobody had anything like that today. Not because it couldn't be done, but it just wasn't safe, and nobody was crazy enough to fund someone trying.

Of course, he was going to be rich.

Was he crazy enough to fly? The technology had existed. People understood it, even, but nobody had built something like that since forever.

You were safer underground than on the surface, to say nothing of being up where the Scour could get hold of you.

Duff had watched the few birds around immediately dive

to the ground and burrow whenever the sky changed. Not all of them presaged the Scour, but he supposed that doing that meant you survived, so birds that didn't weren't around anymore. His team had always done the same, but they'd never faced a big Scour either.

He shook his head at some fanciful silliness. He'd bridge that gap when he got there, and not before.

Lefty emerged now and sat next to him.

"She's asleep," Lefty said. "Those things work quick."

"One would put me to sleep pretty fast," he agreed.

"And now?" she asked.

He could see something in her eyes, but couldn't tell what it was.

Duff took the coward's way out. He rose and put his empty mug on the counter.

"Bed," he said. "We'll be up early and walking a long ways, so best if everyone's rested."

When he turned around, she was standing. Close.

Too close, he thought, but there wasn't much he could say. Nor anywhere to move, as she had him almost backed up against the counter.

She didn't speak. Just studied him.

Duff felt like prey.

She stepped even closer. He was practically breathing on her now.

At least she didn't have a gun in her hand, although he had no doubts one could be there the instant she needed it.

"Duff?" she started, but no more words came.

"Lefty?" he asked, hopelessly lost at the look in her eyes and what she might be trying to say.

"Not Lefty," she whispered. "Harper."

"Harper," he repeated, trying on her new name. Or old one.

Duff wasn't sure what it meant that she wanted to be Harper now, instead of Lefty.

"I'm scared," she continued, stepping even closer.

Duff tentatively put his arms around her, because this lethally-dangerous woman seemed to want him to. Her weight settled against his chest, pressing him back against the counter as her head lay on his shoulder.

"I'm going to do everything I can, Harper," he murmured.

"I know," she whispered.

He felt her arms wrap around his waist.

Fortunately, her heart was going about as fast as his was. He could feel the echoes in his chest.

He was still a coward in some ways. She leaned back and studied him from close enough to breathe on. That was okay, because he'd stopped breathing.

Kissing her, as much fun as it might be, still sounded like a really dumb idea right now.

She seemed to understand that, because after a moment she shifted her weight back some.

The woman was shorter than him, but not that much. Maybe a handful of centimeters. Gorgeous green eyes that looked to see right through him.

"Can I ask a favor?" she probed, voice quiet and careful.

"Sure," he replied, heart still pounding mad.

"Just hold me tonight?" Harper asked him.

Wasn't Lefty. No, that cold-blooded killer was nowhere to be found.

This was Harper. At least the woman she was trying to become.

Who might Duff be, when he couldn't be Duff anymore?

When it wasn't safe to be him?

"Sure," he repeated.

She stepped back, but took his hand in hers and led him to his bunk.

Acheson's bunk.

Theirs?

Duff watched her strip off her boots, spats, gloves, and hat. Left the gunbelt on the chair.

Peeled herself out of that leather top and placed it atop the longcoat.

Looked almost vulnerable as she sat on the bed, otherwise clothed.

He got his boots and coat off. Belt and stuff.

Both of them just in pants and shirt.

He laid down and shifted himself backwards until his butt was against the wall. She pulled the blanket up and shifted into his arms with her back against his belly. His arms went around her almost automatically.

Duff couldn't remember the last time he'd actually slept with a woman, as opposed to paying her for her time and then being on his way. It felt weird but good.

Hopefully she felt the same.

He laid there and listened to the woman breathe. Heard it growing slower and deeper.

Eventually, darkness claimed him.

CHAPTER 25

Red woke in darkness. Night still, outside. Pain brought her to the surface, but it wasn't as bad as it had been.

Sharp, but not debilitating.

Just pain.

She looked at the bunk above her, but it was obvious Lefty wasn't there.

She smiled, pretty sure where the woman was. Hopefully, Duff didn't mind catering to Lefty's fears and foibles.

Red didn't need a man to be fulfilled. They were fun, but unnecessary.

Lefty didn't work that way, but it wasn't Red's problem.

She rose slowly, feeling the bones shift with little stabs she could manage if she was careful. The corset really had saved her life. That and just strapping herself into the chair to be out of everyone's way, physically as well as emotionally.

And keeping the corset on for the last two days had held her together. The bones were knitting.

She didn't know how long she would be able to walk in the morning, but she'd make it. Stamina wouldn't be her problem, because she was at least as stubborn as Lefty, but her body would demand more breaks while it healed.

She had closed the curtain that morning, but opened it when she'd gone to bed. The stars were bright and cold and distant as she looked up. Raw dirt and stone stretched out in front of her into the distance.

The moon was almost full overhead, so it must be getting on to morning now, if she understood the old rules about telling time based on the phases.

It felt so weird to be on the surface where you could see those things. Only the SkyFolk and their close friends got to stay under the domes, back in Levin. Everyone else went to sleep with stone overhead.

Red wondered what Brigadoon would be like. As a little girl, there had been stories, but she'd always dismissed them as fanciful. A whole underground fastness hidden in the desert and not connected with the Nine Cities?

Some of the stories talked about wars between two sides. That made more sense, except if the Nine Cities had won, hadn't they destroyed the place afterwards? Or at least thought they had?

If there were ruins left behind, maybe someone had snuck back in later and fixed things up? The place was supposed to be a criminal haven, so that made more sense.

What frightened her was the new man they were hanging their fates on. Lefty would bond with him like she had Matthias before. The woman was broken, but not in bad ways. She just didn't have any dreams or motivation of her own, and needed someone else to supply them.

If it was a man who could satisfy her other needs, then Lefty was all set. Duff would probably keep her around for that reason. What man didn't like having a sidekick who was generally passive and pretty loud in bed?

Red had no intention of joining them. Or even just him while Lefty was elsewhere. She had gold, at least for now.

God only knows what would happen when they got where they were going.

If they got to where they were going.

Red could see being odd-girl-out with the other two. Needing to walk away at the drop of one of Lefty's pretty hats, and vanish into the darkness of a tunnel. She had skills that probably weren't very useful at Brigadoon, but might convince someone to hire her.

Maybe even take her back to the Nine Cities to do some jobs.

Or could she just retire?

Amelia *Red* Zhu was a wanted woman. An escaped felon with a price on her head. No place in the Nine Cities was going to be safe for her.

Should she just live out her time in Brigadoon, if it really existed, with whatever gold the other two let her have? She had enough right now to live a comfortable existence for years if she was prudent.

Duff was planning to bury the rest somewhere along the way. Would he give her her cut when he went back for it? Would Lefty?

Did she need to sneak back out after everything was settled and dig up the box? Take her portion and rebury it?

Red wished she'd been able to work with those two over the last two days. So much had changed about both of them. She didn't know Duff at all, but Lefty had almost become another woman.

What did that presage?

Did she need to kill both of them at some point, before they did her? She didn't think Lefty was that devious, but the man was a dangerous stranger in this industry, in spite of soft touch.

Red returned to the bunk and settled carefully, working on her breathing as a way to loosen up everything enough she could sleep.

In a few hours, she was going to walk across the desert floor, possibly with a pair of what had been complete strangers before.

Would they still be after this?

CHAPTER 26

Harper woke warm and cuddly. It was a strange feeling, because Matthias hated being touched when he slept. It woke him up.

Yet the man had his arms around her, purring quietly in her ear as he was pressed against her. One hand was around her stomach, while the other held her hand under the pillow.

She smiled, and then realized that Matthias was dead. She'd seduced Duff last night.

At least as much as she thought he was capable of handling right now.

What kind of a man was afraid of a forward woman?

Trick question. When pressed, most of them folded, unwilling to really go there.

They wanted someone pliant and sexy who would hang out with them, but not make any difficult demands, like getting settled into a job where you weren't on the run constantly, or getting married and starting a family.

Harper didn't think she wanted kids. Her mother had certainly regretted the whole process. And her father...

The less said, the better.

The authorities had never found that son of a bitch's body, but she'd made sure he never touched another young girl.

Harper listened to Duff breathe.

He wasn't frightened of her. She'd seen that in his eyes.

Duff was afraid of failure. Of letting her and Red down. Getting one of them killed by making some stupid mistake.

Maybe of walking right up to a door at Brigadoon and knocking, knowing that he might never be allowed to leave again.

His breathing changed and she knew he was awake. Harper wondered if his unconscious had known she was up, and brought him to the surface. She'd known people like that. They couldn't sleep well next to a stranger, so it took time for them to be comfortable.

Duff didn't act like someone that had spent a lot with a pretty woman in his arms.

She rolled inside his arms, accidentally booping noses with him as she shifted.

"Didn't mean to wake you," he said.

"I was awake, listening to you sleep," Harper replied, astounding herself that it was the truth, and that she'd tell him something like that.

"You okay?" he asked her, trying to stare into her eyes from too close.

"Nervous," she said.

More truth. What had come over her? Who was she?

Harper.

Someone she hadn't been in over a decade. Not since she was maybe eleven years old.

Who was Duff to bring all this to the surface again?

Harper didn't have answers.

"The desert will just be tough and slow," he assured her.

"Nothing exotic there. If some animal does bother us, I presume you're a pretty good shot. It's Brigadoon that worries me."

"I'll take care of you," she said, surprising herself but unable to retract the words.

She wasn't sure she wanted to, either.

"And Red," she went on, cementing the three of them as a team, like the Matthias's people had been, just two days ago.

"Never dealt with criminals in a group before," Duff whispered.

"We're just as crazy as normal people," Harper smiled, feeling his hand close on the small of her back, below her bra, where the heat penetrated her shirt and warmed her skin.

"You going to become a crime boss?" he asked in a teasing voice.

"Not me," Harper replied. "Red, either. But I could turn you into one, if you wanted."

"Never," Duff said, shivering. "I don't know if I can ever return to Levin or one of those places, but I'd like to keep living quiet, wherever I end up."

"Me, too," she said, wondering at what was coming over her.

Wasn't love. At least she didn't think so. But Harper was going to turn out a different woman than Lefty ever had.

She would still need Lefty. Need to be ready to kill someone at the drop of a hat, or over an insult in a bar.

But she could also go someplace quiet with Duff and be Harper, too.

"If you can't be you, what should I call you?" she asked, leaning back just a little so his whole face was visible.

She watched him almost go through the stages of death.

"Dunno," he finally said. "My real name is Torcuil, which meant Thor's Kettle in one of the ancient languages."

"How about I call you Thor, then?" she smiled tentatively.

"That might work, Harper," he said. "Pleased to meet you."

"You, too, Thor," she said.

Just because, she kissed him. It wasn't passionate or sloppy. Just a quick peck to say hello. And maybe set the stage for something more interesting when they needed to celebrate making it into Brigadoon safely and having the rest of their lives ahead of them.

Tomorrow was going to be an adventure.

Duff wasn't used to thinking of himself even as Torcuil, let alone Thor. He'd been Duff since he was sixteen, and working around Thorstein Dubhthaigh, his father and everybody else's boss.

Everyone had taken to calling him Duff, and that had been his name for almost as long as this beautiful woman in his arms had been alive.

She slept now, facing him and drooling a little on his arm.

He could feel the sunrise coming. The sky was just starting to lighten up as he watched the distant mountains of Death. Stars were slowly fading over there.

What the hell. Time to wake up.

He gave Harper just enough of a shift to open those eyes.

She came back from far away and centered on him.

"It's time," he said simply.

Another change came over her. Harper vanished back into the depths and Lefty returned.

Even her breathing shifted into a new pattern.

"Okay," she said, rolling away and standing in silence.

Duff joined her. The cabin was too small for two people, but he didn't mind when she brushed up against him.

After a moment, however, he sat back down and watched her gear up. The corset. The gunbelt. Boots. Spats. Hat. Gloves. Longcoat.

Lefty looked down at him, but it was Harper that smiled.

They traded places and he got everything ready.

"I'll make coffee while you got check on Red," he said, opening the door quietly.

If only there was some way to haul the refrigerator with him. Duff had no idea where the batteries or power were, and it was too big anyway, but cold juice would be helpful on a long trip across the hot desert floor.

He settled for refilling all the canteens he'd been able to find. That would be a lot of the weight he and Lefty carried, at least initially. Plus what they could put inside themselves to sweat out. Most of Red's gear was being left behind, and Lefty would carry her nearly-empty backpack in addition the mail bag.

Duff would still have most of the load.

Red emerged, looking better than she had since he'd first laid eyes on her.

She even smiled at him, but it was a secret kind of smile, and he felt himself blushing for reasons he didn't fully understand.

Not a novel experience around a woman. Especially not a smart one, like both of these two.

Breakfast was the heaviest stuff he could find, cans of corned beef hash with a lot of salt. They would need salt crossing the sun.

The false dawn was up when they were done.

Duff turned his face to the southeast and measured the

time and the direction. His compass was behaving this morning, but linemen had learned that the Scour made them lie occasionally, and you had to watch the sun as well as the dial.

Red and Lefty were set. Hats on. Scarves around necks and faces. Gloves. Boots. As filled up with water and coffee as they could be and everyone had a good piss before they went.

He stepped down on the desert and handed both women down. Bags got set. Red had taken a quarter pill, and wasn't carrying anything today. Maybe tomorrow, depending, but healed was better than fast.

Duff took one end of the gold and Lefty the other. It was lighter, minus thirty of the fifteen hundred coins, but that didn't make it light. Still, that was the difference between arriving at Brigadoon as a refugee and a player.

"We can do this, right?" Red asked.

"If we stay, even today, there is a good chance that a line crew down from Olanchas, or up from Capazon, finds the wreck and rescues us," Duff replied. "Then the two of you end up in prison forever as train robbers and I go back to the world where someone hires train robbers like you to kill me one of these days."

"Thank you for doing this, Duff," Red nodded. "Or rather, Thor. I should get used to calling you that so I don't mess up later. And you, too, Harper."

"You got a name, Red?" Lefty asked.

"I was born Amelia," she said. "But nobody has called me that in a long time."

"Even better," Duff offered. "Maybe you can keep being Amelia when we get where we're going."

"Where are we going, Thor?" Amelia asked. Or maybe Red. Hard to tell.

Something about her tone caused Duff to look at her closer. Lefty did, too.

Red wasn't asking a simple question. The kind that had a simple answer.

Brigadoon, if they survived open desert, whatever wind, heat, or storms came along in the meantime.

She meant after that.

"I don't know, Amelia," Duff replied as honestly as he could. "Supposedly, we'll have enough money when we arrive to live well for a long while, while we figure everything out. And then maybe we can go back and get the rest of the gold once we think we're safe. What do you want, once we're out of the desert?"

"I don't know, Thor," she said. "Been thinking about it, and I have no answers. You two a thing now?"

It was a crude, almost rude question. He blushed.

Glancing over, Lefty was blushing as well. Duff didn't think Lefty blushed, but maybe that was Harper peeking out.

Lefty spoke up.

"Maybe," the woman offered. "But we're a team, the three of us. All Thor and I did last night was cuddle. I'd like us to keep being a team when we got there, at least until you decide you need to go a different way than I do, or he does."

Duff remained silent, practicing this Thor person he was going to be. It was a thin disguise, but it would at least keep a memory of Duff Dubhthaigh from lingering. Not many people even knew his real name. Fewer knew how to translate it.

Red studied both of them. He and Lefty kept walking, carrying that dead weight between them, so everyone was moving at a slow pace. He had a tent, but wanted to get off the desert floor before he called it a day and settled everyone.

They had to get around the curve of this first mountain,

and they'd be out of sight of any rescue team coming to drag them back to civilization and prison.

And the grave.

"And when we get to that stage?" Red pressed.

"One third of the gold is yours, Amelia," he promised her. "Nothing will change that. You'll know where it's buried. Unless you completely vanish, you'll know when I think it is safe for us to return for more or the rest. We're partners, simple as that."

"Partners?" she asked. "That's all?"

"At the very least," he said. "You'll have to tell me past that, as I'm still new at this crime business and you two are way more expert than I am. And smarter, too. I'm just a dumb lineman who managed to get himself exiled to a railroad job. And then I screwed that up pretty bad on the first day."

Red returned his smile and seemed to relax some. Her shoulders came down as he watched.

Lefty smiled as well, so he must have said something right. Gods of hell knew what it might be, but hey, even blind mice found cheese occasionally.

Red fell into silence. Duff took that as a good sign.

For the longest time, the only sound was three sets of boots crunching on the dirt and stone, and the light breeze that sporadically swirled around them as the heat differentials started to even out.

By mid-morning, it would be uniformly hot, and the wind would die off. At least until some sort of storm caught up with them.

Duff had never heard of two Scours occurring that close together, but he'd also never seen one that bad before. Usually, they topped out at around one hundred kilometers an hour sustained. If you spiked your tent down properly and laid still on the windward side, it would scream at you, but not tumble things loose or carry anyone away.

Certainly not like that monster that had carried away a train. Three hundred kilometers an hour, maybe. Somewhere, someone had a chart showing the wind strength necessary to do that. Usually, that happened when you were dealing with hurricanes coming up the coast too fast to break themselves up as they hit land.

Had this been a hurricane when it was out over the water? Or had a hurricane been coming and the change in air pressure let the Scour get up a head of steam?

Rain would be nice, as opposed to the heat, but not decimeters of it falling in a single day.

Duff could see wadis and canyons as they walked. Places where water could get up a good head of steam and flashflood you right out before you knew what was happening.

"Okay, I need a break," Lefty spoke first.

Duff automatically checked the sky. They'd walked for about an hour already. Slow, but the wreckage of *Postmaster Seventeen* was mostly out of sight around the curve of the mountain. He could see the engine and part of the crew car.

Someone coming down from the north would likely miss them. At least until they started to move and drew the eye.

Overhead, no birds circled or flew.

Linemen used the birds as a guide, so he wasn't sure what their absence was telling him. In the old days, they fled storms, but here they might not have returned yet.

Still, the sky had been clear and dry. He shifted the women over to a spot that had a slight slope where a dry riverbed emerged and had cut a path. The gold went up on top, but he gestured to the slope.

"That might be cool, still," he offered. "At least until afternoon sun hits it."

Both women took that as a cue and shifted in, putting their butts and backs on the cooler soil.

Duff found a spot to keep watch south, in case another train or repair car was coming.

The ancient legends spoke of fire-breathing engines that belched a black smoke into the air, letting anyone see them from kilometers off. Batteries and oil-fueled generators meant that the modern machines could sneak up on you.

He focused on the track, but nothing was evident.

Duff felt bad, hoping that the teams were going to be a week fixing track coming from both directions, and that neither would make it here until he and women were safely away.

The alternative was too much to worry about.

Him dead. Them in prison, without anybody to rescue them.

All this because some union boss had gotten a little too greedy, and wanted to cover up his side games rather than just live an honest life?

Duff shook his head.

"What's so interesting?" Red asked.

Amelia. Needed to work on that.

She'd ended up closer of the two. Lefty might have been asleep, as calm and peaceful as she looked.

Duff made sure Lefty's color was still good, so maybe she was just meditating or something.

"Wondering about all the little choices that got us here, Amelia," he replied, studying the woman's face next. "You folks were hired to kill me, because one of my people got too greedy, back home. Now we're all on the run from that person, as well as everyone else. And we're going to go hide with a bunch or criminals."

"Regrets?" she stared at him.

"More than I can possibly list," he shrugged. "But not you two. You'll keep me alive, because had I been the only survivor, I'd have started back to Olanchas instead. That would have just delivered me right into the jaws of my own doom."

"You just don't look like a criminal, Thor," she said carefully. Tentatively, like she was afraid of insulting him.

"I'm not, Amelia," he replied. "Not sure I plan to be. I'm a survivor. So are the two of you. We'll survive this. And hopefully be SkyFolk when we get there. I've been trying to figure out what to do with the second half of my life."

"Ideas?" she asked.

"Men and women used to be able to fly," he shrugged again. "Before the War. Before the Scour. Now we have the rail, but is there a better way to get around? Could we detect a Scour long before it hit and maybe avoid it?"

"So you're a dreamer?" she asked, her face turning serious.

Duff shrugged. He'd been called worse in his time. Linemen didn't generally dream. Too busy most of the time working out how to fix the existing gear and technology, so that nobody fell back to what things had been like when the world first crashed from the Scours. He'd spent most of his time looking down, instead of up.

But yeah, maybe he could dream.

"Maybe," he answered. "You?"

"I've been in and out of reformatories and jails since I was fourteen, Thor," she said. "Not like Lefty. Harper. But the rules and I don't generally fit all that much. Found out that I had a knack for opening any lock you had, so I drifted over into that world. Never got rich, but never meant to. Just wanted pretty things to wear, or being able to prove to someone that I was that good."

"I see," Duff said, still pretending to be Thor. "And when we get there?"

"Like you, I'll have to dream of something else," she shrugged in turn, wincing a little as she did. "Something bigger, maybe. Something at least interesting enough to keep me from getting so bored I start robbing SkyFolk again."

"What's east of Death?" Harper suddenly spoke up, not opening her eyes, but proving that she was awake and had been listening.

Duff thought about it for a second.

"Legend says that the desert was always there, but not as lethal," he replied. "More mountains, and then finally a great grassland that went on for weeks. Maybe more cities burrowed into mountains somewhere past that. Nobody has made it across the desert and mountains that I know of, headed either direction."

"That might be a dream," Harper said.

Duff grunted. There was crazy, and then there was suicidal.

Even flying was risky, but he'd always figured that from up there you'd be able to see a Scour coming and get down to the ground quickly enough to hide.

"No trains," he offered, thinking some more. "No track. You'd need an engine that could just roll across the ground. Electric, because you couldn't haul enough fuel to get anywhere, or be sure you'd find anything when you did. And roads or something."

"Are there roads?" Amelia asked.

It was weird, already thinking of these women by their real names, instead of who everyone else called them, but he'd only barely known Red or Lefty, so Amelia and Harper were people he could begin to understand.

"I don't know," Duff answered instead of Thor. "There were people everywhere, before the war or the Scour, so there must have been. We would sometimes see remains of things when we worked that might have been roads a long time ago. Long, straight scars across the desert floor."

"Maybe I'll have to steal an ancient map," Amelia smiled up at him. "Research, you know?"

Thor smiled back at her. Harper did as well.

"Gonna go commit archaeology when nobody is looking?" he asked her.

"Need to keep the skills sharp," she shrugged eloquently. "And need to keep the team together when we get there."

That struck home. Harper flinched, too.

They would need to have a group effort. Could they somehow cross the empty vastness of the interior and find something?

Someone?

Or was that just a more interesting way to die?

He didn't know.

"Harper, you ready to move some more?" he called. "I'd like to get another kilometer or so if we can, to get fully out of sight. Then we can talk about how far we want to travel today."

She groaned but stood up. Duff lifted Amelia to her feet, rather than making her twist and hurt herself again.

They picked up the big trunk of gold that was the key to so many possible futures and began to waddle forward into the deadly, morning sun.

CHAPTER 28

Red cogitated as she walked.

Thor had insisted that she lead, so that they didn't miss her falling behind when there were so focused on the weight they were carrying.

The suggestion of a map had been a throwaway line. Something to fill an otherwise-empty conversation.

She wasn't a dreamer. That was Thor. Harper, too, maybe, but Lefty had been too lazy to dream. Red had seen that. Matthias had done enough dreaming for the five of them.

But the thought of a map tugged at her. Asked her rude questions about actually finding one.

Going there to see what had survived.

Thor was tough and canny, but not a literate, educated man. That much was clear. At the same time he was also, like he said, a survivor who knew the outdoors better than anyone she'd ever met.

Lefty/Harper was the deadliest person Amelia had ever known.

But Red had studied. You had to, in order to get in somewhere, steal something, and get out safe again. Mistakes had put her in various jails. Failures of planning. Bad luck. Whatever.

So Amelia read. More than Harper did, because she had to study things. Old histories. Family trees. Even blueprints someone had, just so she knew what to steal and what to ignore as bait.

Would there be libraries at Brigadoon?

She doubted it. Career criminals tended to be the kinds of people who sneered at libraries and organization. That was why they became criminals in the first place.

Would they have to return to the Nine Cities to find the bits and pieces that might scratch this sudden itch that had taken hold right in the middle of her back?

She'd planned to stop being a thief. But maybe, just maybe, she needed to remain one if she wanted to be an explorer. Thor was handy. Harper deadly. Amelia could be sneaky.

Something tugged at her mind as she walked, lost in dreams not of avarice, but of legend.

Lines.

Straight squareness in the middle of the desert floor.

"Hey," she said, calling out loud enough that the others stopped before they ran her over with that mass of gold.

Both set it down at the slightest suggestion of a break. Thor automatically turned to study the southwestern horizon for movement, but he'd been doing that as they walked, always fearful that rescuers were coming.

Fearful for her and Harper.

That was a new thing in her life, too. Amelia wasn't sure how to think about it.

At the moment, she had other issues.

"What is it?" Harper asked as she stepped close.

Amelia held out a hand and pointed at the land in front of them.

It wasn't obvious close, but when you were looking a ways off, it was clear.

"This is a road of some sort," she said. "Wider than a railroad, but straight. See?"

Thor had turned at her words and stepped up on her other side.

"Wow," he muttered. "You're right."

It was raised a little from the rest of the floor, like someone had scraped out both sides and then packed everything down with a heavy weight.

The Scour was wind. Earthquakes had broken up the ground and moved some things around, but no grit or dirt had accumulated enough to obscure the line running away from them straight across the desert floor.

Walking would certainly be easier, but they would be out in the open. At least during the day.

"Harper?" she turned to the woman. "Where are we on your map?"

Harper reached into that inside pocket where she kept the interesting papers and pulled the bundle out.

Amelia took the opportunity to sit down on the box with the gold, just because she could.

Healing wasn't the same as healed, and she didn't know how much farther Thor wanted to take them today.

Harper and Thor consulted. It seemed to involve a lot of muttering and pointing, but she just continued to watch the horizon like Thor had been doing.

Movement caused her to gasp.

"What?" Harper asked, suddenly turning back into the

deadly gunslinger known as Lefty, one pistol out and head turning back and forth.

"Stop moving," Amelia snapped at the woman. "Stand perfectly still."

Both of them froze.

Amelia watched the movement begin to resolve itself. There was a train coming.

Slowly, like it was feeling its way along the tracks, but the giant, black snake slithered along the railroad line anyway.

"Company," she said simply.

Lefty and Duff turned to see it. Harper and Thor were gone, just like that.

The distance to the train was vast, and the rails apparently turned some, because the train was just coming into sight around a curve as she watched.

"Down, but slowly," Duff ordered.

Both of them squatted. Amelia slipped off her box and laid flat on the hot ground behind it, hoping that her blue and black jacket had picked up enough dust to not stand out.

"Do we run?" she asked in a normal voice.

"We can't run with all that gold," Harper replied tartly.

"I'm aware of that," Amelia said. "Would you rather be free or rich?"

"We'll have a chance to be both," Duff spoke up now. "They'll stop a little closer to the wreck, and be out of sight from here. When they disappear, we'll move, skirting closer to the mountain until we can find a spot to put up the tent for today."

That sounded good to Amelia. She was tired of being Red. Tired of being a criminal. She'd just gotten her head around being an explorer instead.

Those bastards over there didn't get to ruin it for her.

The sun pounded down on her. She pulled the cloth up to completely cover her face. It wasn't much, but every little bit helped. Amelia could taste the water being sucked out of her body by the heat and what little breeze was dying down.

"Thor, will they be able to follow us?" she asked, turning her head that way. "Track us across the desert floor?"

"It's all stone," he replied. "Unless they saw us just now, there shouldn't be anything they can follow. We did leave evidence of being there this morning, but I don't know how hard they'll search."

"Do we move as soon as we can, bury the gold here, and then try to disappear?" she continued.

"Maybe," was all he could offer her.

Well, she supposed that they could just wait here, and then get into a gunfight with those folks if they did come this way. That would drive them off pretty quickly, but Amelia also presumed that they'd come back with help.

Maybe bring real trackers who could follow them across the desert. Find the gold and take it back.

That would never do.

"Okay, they're out of sight." Thor was up.

He stood over her and put his hands under her shoulders. It hurt to be lifted this way, but the alternative was even worse, so she gritted her teeth and let him get her upright.

They all had an extra oomph in their step now. Fear of prison would do that to anyone.

Thor pointed her in the right direction and she started walking, knowing that even with the gold they could catch her quickly enough.

There was a small canyon just beyond where they'd

stopped. Possibly something originally cut by water than had fallen from the sky and then widened over time by wind. Very little vegetation, mostly clumps of grass that Duff had warned everyone to avoid, as the things that most likely lived in places like that and would bite or sting.

Behind her, she heard the two of them lurch along.

Amelia got to the place where the walls turned sideways and started to open up. She moved deeper, looking for cover, but this little gap was south-facing, so it would be in the direct sun all day.

"Good enough," Thor called after she had gone a bit in.

The ground started upward here, and she didn't want to know if she could ascend any kind of steep slope. The other two dropped the box and Amelia more or less collapsed, feeling like she had just run here instead of briskly walking.

Harper drew a pistol and watched for followers, while Thor dropped his bag and dug out a bundle that he unfolded into a tent by adding a series of flexible posts that bent into a U-shape.

"In you go," he said, only three minutes later.

Amelia hated moving like an old lady, but she had no choice today. At least it got her out of the sun. Thor began closing it up.

"What about you two?" she asked, confused.

"We're better protected against the sun," Harper called quietly. "Plus, I need to be ready to drive them off. Thor, do we dig here?"

She listened as they spoke. Even though they were just a meter away, the wall of slick material between then made it seem like the veil between worlds. The tent had clear, plastic windows on both sides, so she could see, but still.

"This might be as good as any place," Amelia offered. "We were about to mark ourselves on the map when trouble arrived. And we'll move faster without it. Then you're just slowed down by me."

Thor grunted and stepped to where Harper was watching.

"Can I see the map?" he asked.

She handed it to him and Amelia watched him study it like a holy relic.

Buried treasure, as it were.

About to be buried, anyway.

Harper kept watch. Amelia decided she was in enough pain that it was cutting through the medicine, so she laid flat to listen.

"That road is on this map, I think," he said. "Here. Wouldn't have recognized it but for walking it. So the canyon would be here, and we should be able to remember it, since this was the one big one facing south. I think digging is a good idea."

"Works for me," Harper chimed in.

"Yes," Amelia said.

It would take some time, but they couldn't cross the open while there was a rescue train there, unless they deviated to the north far enough to get below the horizon.

If they could. And could lose any pursuers.

"Thor, with the train destroyed, would they try to salvage it, or just fix the rails and return to their base?" Amelia asked as she heard the man start rooting around in his bag.

Presumably, going for the shovel she'd seen him pack.

"I don't know, Red," he replied.

"Amelia," she corrected him. They needed to stay in character.

"Amelia," he repeated.

She listened as he dug, cursing quietly under his breath as he worked. Harper presumably kept watch.

Amelia let the heat and stress and pain lull her into something like resting.

She slept.

CHAPTER 29

Harper. Even with a gun in her hand, she needed to remember to be Harper, and not Lefty.

Thor was digging. Amelia was resting in the tent out of the sun. The world had changed.

Harper was keeping watch, hoping that no snakes suddenly emerged from their dens.

She would shoot first and then worry about the sound carrying far enough to bring railroad cops after her.

They weren't taking her in. She had enough ammunition to settle that conversation, at least until they went back and brought a whole bunch of friends.

She could suddenly see a future that didn't involve her just being someone's deadly moll, and wasn't about to let anyone take that away from her.

And Amelia had brought it up instead of Thor. Wonder of wonders.

"Amelia, where would we find a map?" she asked loud enough for the woman to answer, but nobody did.

She snuck over and listened as Amelia breathed too regularly to be awake. She peeked in, but Amelia had covered her face with the cloth and left it.

"Should we wake her?" Harper asked Thor quietly as he worked.

He paused and stepped close, listening.

"She sounds okay," he said. "Just exhausted. Let me do this and then we'll check, but you keep listening to her breathe."

"Okay," Harper nodded and moved to a spot next to the tent where she could sit on the rise of the wall.

Had the rest of the world survived?

Supposedly, the Scour didn't do the same things over water that it did over land, but hurricanes were supposedly way more common now than before. And bigger and deadlier.

Nobody lived on the coast anymore, except down where the California gulf had climbed clear up into the desert.

Harper had read a book written back when Angels was a place, rather than underwater. Like Palm Springs and the Salton Sea.

There were even rumors that people lived above ground, way to the north where the Scours weren't as bad. Beyond Power or Senna, where you had to worry about volcanoes instead.

Was the north safer? Better? More interesting?

Less likely to prosecute and extradite?

Things a girl needed to know.

"Need your help," Thor suddenly spoke up.

She'd been paying attention to the distance and Amelia breathing, and lost track of the man and his hole. But it was done.

Done enough. Either nobody was around, or people would be coming after them.

Not a lot of other options.

Harper holstered her pistol and grabbed the other end of the heavy box.

She had images in her head of the old days, when people were buried in the ground, rather than cremated to make fertilizer for crops. More things from her old books.

At least she had remembered to steal one of Acheson's books before she left.

Well, inherit, maybe. Hard to tell. Nobody would miss it, and it would give her and Thor something extra to remember him by, in addition to all that gold.

And their lives, assuming they could get out of this mess.

Down into the hole it went. Thor shifted it over onto its side and then began pushing dirt back in. She moved back and watched, wondering when it would next see sunlight.

She wasn't feeling morbid or anything, but things happened.

"Hang on," she said, interrupting him.

Harper got down on her knees and managed to tilt the box up. She popped the latch and reached inside, grabbing one more sleeve of coins before she closed everything back up.

"Three for you. Three for Amelia. Three for me. One for luck and bribes," she offered.

He didn't say anything. Just shrugged and went back to work.

But Thor was a worker, not a criminal. Not a killer.

He would need her to kill anyone threatening them, because he might not just shoot some stupid bastard through the heart if they decided to get obnoxious.

Not like her. Either Lefty or Harper.

Both were killers, just for different reasons.

Fast enough, it was gone. Just a damp spot in the canyon floor that would dry out quickly. Thor had smoothed it out, but now he piled rocks atop it. It didn't look natural, but if you were looking for something here, you already knew what, and just needed to know where.

Hopefully, the first big rain wouldn't wash it all away, forcing them to spend all day or all week camped here and digging.

Harper stepped back and tried to imprint the whole space in her memory, for when they came back. Get it all so they could be in and out and gone.

"Now what?" she asked when he folded his shovel back up and stashed it in the bag.

"Now, we wait," he answered.

She was good at that, so she found a comfortable spot where she could watch for intruders and listen to Amelia sleeping. She pulled three coins from the sleeve and handed them to Thor. Three went into secret little pouches on her corset, behind straps that she used to adjust its tightness from day to day.

Four she held onto for Amelia.

In the distance, the heat shimmered, but nobody appeared.

Eventually, the sun passed the rim of the mountains and they were in shadow.

CHAPTER 30

He'd waited all day, but nobody had arrived from that train to cast him into oblivion. Near as Duff could tell, that meant that it was time for him to stop being Duff and start living as Thor for the rest of his life.

Or at least until the three of them acquired new identities somehow and could live someplace safe. With several million people in the Nine Cities, plus the hope of others living in Brigadoon, there had to be a way he could do this.

Or a place he could go.

But Duff was done.

Thor watched the sun slowly setting with ambivalent eyes. There would be enough moonlight later that they could walk some more, but he had no idea what creatures might have been hiding during the day and ready to come out now.

Camels? Elephants? Tigers?

Nothing bothered a line crew, but they also made noise and kept a couple of the gandy dancers awake all night with rifles. Plus the lights from the train if it was handy.

Amelia had napped off and on, but that was to be

expected. She was actually looking mostly healed now, having climbed out of the tent to sit next to him, on the other side from Harper as they ate some more food.

He was in the middle again. Hopefully, that was just an accident.

"We should pack up and get some more distance while we can," he said tentatively, waiting for either woman to disagree.

Instead, both rose silently and stretched.

Thor took that as a sign and quickly broke the tent down and rolled it up. He could get grit and any bugs out later, when they were ready to settle for the night.

It went into his bag, and the rifle came out. He assembled it quickly enough, and then slipped eight cartridges into the cylinder. Very little of the weapon was actually metal, beyond the primers and lead bullets themselves. The design was just an oversized revolver, holding eight instead of six with a strap to go over your shoulder.

He handed it to Harper.

"Same bullets as yours," he said. "Longer barrel, in case you have to shoot something. More likely to kill it.

"What's out here at night?" Harper asked.

Obviously, she'd been wondering the same things he had.

"Dunno," he replied honestly. "But I'd rather you killed it first, whatever it was."

She nodded, sobering, and checked the weapon with a professional eye.

Thor turned to Amelia and she nodded. Smiled even. Had only taken two quarter pills today, so either she was tougher than he was, or healing faster than he did.

Either way was good.

Thor had memorized the track, with not much better to do with his time this afternoon while he was keeping watch for a posse. He led for now, with Amelia following and Harper guarding the rear.

He had his pistol if anything came near, but a gunshot would echo forever in this landscape and eventually trouble would come for them on two legs.

Lots of trouble.

Instead of worrying, he watched the ground and let the fading sunlight guide him. Ahead, the moon was just rising over the horizon, shimmering like a pearl under water.

The ancient road Amelia had seen stood out. It was a different shade than the dirt around it. Maybe ram-packed gravel originally. Possibly treated with something to make it hold together after all this time.

Without much rain to break it down, any material designed for heat would last. Scours would keep dirt from drifting up and burying it.

Thor could see where an ancient earthquake had cracked the floor and shifted everything, but it hadn't turned into one of those man-eating chasms, like they did in the bad vids he watched when he was home.

The heat was starting to fade without the terrible sun over-head. A breeze would come up soon, blowing things southerly like they did at night.

It would be bitterly cold in a few hours, but he had thermal blankets packed for just this emergency, and both women had enough layers on to retain heat.

He walked, eyes looking for any sort of monster suddenly emerging from the ground and charging, like happened in horror movies.

The only dangerous thing on the desert floor tonight appeared to be the two women with him.

Good enough.

Something howled in the distance, long and mournful. South of them somewhere, but not close.

Maybe the train folk would keep things at a distance by making too much ruckus.

Something else answered that howl. This one was north.

"Are we being hunted?" Harper asked.

"I have no idea," Thor replied. "Let's pick up the pace a little and see if we can get someplace with cover."

They agreed, and Thor began to walk faster, eyes going back and forth.

At the bottom of this narrower valley, the ground had indeed moved. It looked like someone had torn a piece of paper, and then taped the two pieces back together, but not quite lined up.

The road he was following was almost a hand-span shifted to the left across that line.

When had that happened? It didn't look recent, so Brigadoon should still be there.

Assuming it was ever there, at the end of this path.

When had he started to assume the place existed, instead of just being a fable parents told their children about?

About the same time that he realized someone had paid that mastermind and his crew an awful lot of gold just to kill one fireman.

Now, he was running away from the folks that would happily rescue him and take him home to Levin.

The howls were closer. Maybe.

Or just louder.

Coming this way? Or was he so wound up right now that everything seemed worse?

Thor paused and took a deep breath. Dumbest thing he

could do right now was sprain an ankle tripping over something. Unless he managed to break a leg out here.

Then the women would have to get him help.

And maybe start running as soon as the line team came into sight.

"They're getting closer," Harper called in a low, tight voice.

Thor drew his pistol and watched the terrain.

Helped that everything was a sandy, dirty color as the moonlight washed colors out. Anything dark would stand out.

Anything moving would draw someone's fire and there would be a lot of it.

Howls lit up the night. Dog-like yips now, but Thor didn't know if that was excitement at finding new prey, or lonesomeness given voice.

Suddenly, a gunshot rang out across the desert, but it wasn't close.

Behind them, somewhere.

Thor still fell into a jog for about a dozen steps before his brain engaged and he realized what he'd heard.

He slowed down, and Amelia ran smack into his back. He turned and caught her as she stumbled.

Harper was close behind.

"Something chasing us?" she asked, spinning around and aiming her rifle into the darkness.

A second shot filled the night. Then several more.

Sounded like thunder, muffled and distant.

"Someone at the lineman camp got spooked," Thor guessed. "Fired at something. Maybe a critter got too close. Maybe just seeing ghosts at the edge of the campfire."

The night fell silent again as they waited and listened.

Thor looked at the ridge of mountains and escarpments

about them. The map showed what had been his original target, but they'd gotten onto the road and then wandered off when a second, ancient road crossed it, this one headed straight east.

Ahead of him, a pair of smaller rocks emerged, stuck out from the end of a ridgeline running to the southeast and dividing the larger valley off from their destination, the legendary Brigadoon.

He turned to Amelia, close in the night beside him.

"How are you doing?" he asked.

"Just ran, and it barely hurt," she replied, gasping a little, but that was probably adrenaline more than anything.

He turned and pointed at the pair of peaks in the dark distance.

"Think you can make it there, if we just walk normal and pay attention for anything the railroad crew chased off?"

"I can try," she said in that particular tone of voice a woman got when she was going to prove she could outlast you at something.

Thor checked his compass against the moon. Everything seemed to be on line, so maybe the last of the previous Scour had passed and things would be good for a time. He had moonlight, and they were moving faster than he'd originally planned, since there was no gold weighing them down right now.

"Harper?" he asked the other shadow.

"The sooner we cross, the sooner we can find the future," she replied, just like a character out of a vid being all prophetic and stuff.

"Good enough," Thor decided aloud. "We'll make it there tonight and find a place to hole up and camp while we see what the others do in the sun tomorrow."

He started by putting one foot in front of the other, trying to keep his head up and watch for trouble ahead.

The desert floor was almost as flat as a hallway, carved back into the deep stone of Levin. Even when they crossed an area of wash and tumble from ancient times, the road was above it all.

The moon was behind him when the roadway slanted to the left again. He took the track, but only went maybe half a kilometer before he turned and left the roadway behind. The ground got rougher here, so he had to slow down, but the surge of stuff in his gut carried him and he had to slow down from time to time when Amelia or Harper said something.

Eventually, he was standing between the two little peaks.

The one on his left was a sharp spike, like he drove to hold ties down, while the ground on his right got rough. Happily, there was a little rise between the two. Not much, but it had a nice saddle and space on the back where he could set a tent and be out of the sun for much of the day.

And out of sight in case anybody from that train decided to wander over this way looking for survivors.

"Are we there yet?" Amelia asked in a voice that couldn't mask her exhaustion.

"There's a bit of a slope to climb," Thor pointed. "We can circle to the left and come up a flat spot, but that's the best place to be right now."

"Go," she growled. "I'll make it."

He hoped so. They'd crossed this entire area in one night, when he'd expected it to take two. Hell, come nightfall they might make it to the door to Brigadoon with just a few more hours walking.

Then they'd have to figure out how to knock.

That would be tomorrow's problem. He had enough water to get them there safe with leftovers, as well as food.

He climbed by moonlight. It was harder going, as the moon was about to set in the west. False dawn was coming, but there would be a stretch of time with nothing but starlight overhead and he wanted to be someplace safer by then.

Something glinted in the dirt and sand by his foot as he climbed.

"Hang on," he said just barely above a whisper.

Amelia had her little pistol out now. Harper had the rifle and Thor heard the sound of the hammer coming back and locking.

Dare he?

Yes.

Scorpions and other things got big and mean out here, but he wanted to see what it was down there.

Quickly, Thor moved his bag around front and opened up one of the side pouches to pull out a pocketflash.

Shielding it as much as he could with his body, Thor pointed the light at the ground and turned it on, pistol in his other hand ready to hammer at something if it moved.

Nope.

Huh.

Thor holstered his pistol and reached out with a gloved hand, catching the thing and lifting it.

"What is it?" Amelia asked.

"A button off somebody's jacket," Thor said, looking at the path ahead of them.

Maybe he hadn't been the first person to look at this terrain and decide it made a good place to keep watch?

He turned to the two women.

"There might be someone or something up top," he said quietly.

"You any good at sneaking?" Amelia asked in a tone he could only qualify as professional.

"No, ma'am," Thor answered honestly.

She glanced back at Harper and something passed between the women, as Harper suddenly let the hammer on the rifle down carefully and handed it to him.

"You wait here," the deadly gunslinger said as she drew one of her pistols, leaving the other hand free.

Thor nodded and the two women seemed to disappear like shadows melting in sunlight.

Within just a few moments, he was completely alone, like Amelia and Harper had just been figments of his imagination all this time. The kind that had carried him this far across the desert.

That was just silly talk.

Right?

A commotion up ahead sounded like voices raised in anger, but no shots fired, which was good.

"Thor?" Harper called in a voice just loud enough to carry to him. "It's safe. Come on up."

Safe?

Thor nodded to himself that at least the women weren't ghosts, and followed them up the track.

He found them at the top of the rise, just about where he'd planned to put a tent.

Except that it would be crowded, as there was already one there.

And a man standing to one side.

With another man seated next to him, holding his hand like it was in pain.

In the moonlight, Thor could see that the one had a belt for a gun, but no gun in it. The seated man as well.

"What's going on?" Thor asked, confused.

"That's what I want to know, pal," the standing man growled back. "Who are you people?"

"We're looking for Brigadoon," Amelia said, matter of factly.

"Well, you found us, lady."

CHAPTER 31

Harper kept the two men covered. Amelia had taken their pistols and moved off to one side. Both men had looked as though they might get stupid enough that she had to shoot at least one of them, at least until Thor arrived, holding that big, black rifle in his hands and looking angry.

She could see that he was actually anxious, but it would look close enough to rage in the darkness, and he was bigger than either of these men.

That size would count a lot.

"What's going on?" Thor's voice sounded confused.

"That's what I want to know, pal," the standing man replied. He'd been on watch until Amelia put a pistol in his ear. "Who are you people?"

"We're looking for Brigadoon," her partner said.

"Well, you found us, lady."

"Not according to the map, we haven't," Harper snapped harshly at the man. She gestured with her free hand. "This was a layover so we could sleep during the day and make it tomorrow."

"You've got a map?" the seated man suddenly perked up. "Where'd you get that?"

"Shut up, Gus," the standing man turned to his partner and looked like he wanted to say something more.

The sound of Thor drawing back the hammer on his rifle filled the night with ominous overtones.

"How about you sit down next to your friend?" Thor suggested in a voice that wasn't going to be polite much longer. "I'm beginning to feel a bit nervous around you folk."

As in: *sit down and shut up, before I have to shoot you.*

Harper had never seen Thor as the man he'd been a week or a year ago, back when he worked the line, but that figure came to the fore now.

Big, tough, and rugged. All the things that had caught her attention when she first drew down on him, but now it was on her side.

The meanness he communicated was probably hollow, since she'd seen the gooey insides of man more than once over the last two days.

Still, she smiled at Gus.

"We were given a map, and passwords," Harper told the other man as the first planted his butt. "Matthias was killed in the storm, but the rest of us made it this far."

"You were out in the storm?" Gus's eyes got big.

"On the train," Amelia spoke up, completing the thought just as Harper had it. "The winds tumbled that damned thing clear across the valley in pieces. You heard the shooting earlier?"

"We did," Gus nodded. "Saw the repair train stop. That them shooting?"

"That's my guess," Harper picked up the thread again. "Wild animals or something, Maybe just night terrors."

"But you three walked right across the desert floor in the middle of the night?" the other man asked, shocked.

"Not my first night out under the stars," Thor growled. "Used to be a lineman, back in the bad old days."

Harper smothered the smile. Bad old days like two months ago?

It made a useful cover, though. She could always introduce him as Thor Lonagan to strangers. She wasn't sure if anybody had even known the tall man's first name. He was just Lonagan, same as Pedro might not have even had a last name.

She could see how the play might go down if they ran into the man who had originally dealt with Matthias.

It would work, too, which was probably the weirdest part.

"So you're looking for the city?" the first man asked.

It was obvious that he was supposed to be in charge. Gus looked more like a helpful puppy than anything, maybe a decade younger and less rough. Barely old enough to shave.

"That's right," Harper said. "Since you two are here, you can escort us."

"We're supposed to be on guard," Gus said.

"And doing a fine job of it, since we snuck right up and took your guns away from you," Harper said. "And I'm not really feeling the need to give them back and maybe have you and your friend shoot us, so either we can keep them and keep going, or you can join us and lead the way. What'll it be, boys."

"How do we know you aren't spies from the Nine Cities?" the older man asked.

"I'd have probably already shot you," Amelia spoke up from the man's side, snapping his head around sharply. "Or just cut your throat to keep everything quiet."

Harper could tell that these boys had never been around

real women. The tough kind who've survived the nastiness that the world might throw at them. Probably just wives and whores, neither of which were likely to give them a good impression, since both of these men looked to be scrapings from the bottom of the barrel.

"So do you want to walk now, or wait until sundown?" Harper asked politely, still aiming her pistol at the older man.

Gus would be amenable to whatever she asked, if she ended up having to shoot his dumbass partner. She'd known men like that.

Most men were like that, after you've demonstrated a callous disregard for life.

"Our relief will be here around dawn," the older man said carefully.

Harper checked the sky and nodded.

"Perfect," she announced. "We'll wait and then you can lead us."

They sat, two disarmed watchers guarded by three twitchy train-robbers.

Harper heard steps coming up the same trail she'd ascended and nodded to Amelia before stepping into cover.

Two sets of boots crunching on the soil. The sun was lighting the eastern sky, but not over yet. The moon was gone

"Hey, Barnett, what's going on?" a voice asked.

Harper stepped out of the darkness and pointed both her pistols at two newcomers who were suddenly caught in a crossfire.

"Morning, boys," she called sweetly. "There was some confusion last night, and my friends and I are a little nervous, so please don't do anything that makes me kill all four of you right now."

The men spun around. One hand went to a holster, but

stopped there when Harper drew a hammer back and centered it on the man.

"I will kill you first," she promised in a flat tone. "And won't miss."

He froze. That hand detached from the butt of his pistol most politely and he stood up a little straighter.

"What's going on?" he asked carefully.

"We're headed to Brigadoon," Harper replied. "Gus and his friend will escort us, and you two can take over their watch.

"The Scavenger will be pissed," he replied. "Armed folks aren't allowed in."

She had no idea who the Scavenger might be, and didn't really care. At this point, there were only two ways forward.

Well, three, if she shot all of them dead, but that would probably make their boss even angrier. At least initially.

"We don't want trouble," Thor spoke up. "How about you boys escort us in and then someone can bring Gus and his friend back their guns? That way you're armed and we don't look like we've got hostages. And someone can chat with them later about letting two pretty girls sneak up on your watchers and take their sidearms away."

Harper suppressed a snort. Thor was probably going to have enemies of the first two by making them out as fools, but that couldn't be helped in this situation. And showing up with the second pair would help defuse things.

She hoped.

Again, four dead men was always an option.

The two newcomers surveyed things with a careful eye, but there wasn't anything much they could do right now.

The one that was looking at her nodded, mostly to himself. And didn't do anything stupid.

"I'm Wilkins," he said to her. "Xi, let's do it their way for now. Gus, don't let Barnett get eaten by a bobcat or anything, okay?"

Wilkins didn't wait for an answer. He started walking down the slope again with his own partner. Harper followed, listening for the sounds of Amelia and Thor behind her.

Or gunshots, if those boys couldn't take no for an answer.

The sun was throwing enough light now that she could keep track of the two men. As long as they stayed ahead of her, there wouldn't be a problem.

After all, she could drop both of them if they decided to split, thinking she'd turn one way of the other.

Besides, all that kind of stunt guaranteed with any other shooter was that one of them died anyway. Here, it would be both.

Amelia caught up with her, moving faster downhill. Harper glanced back and watched Thor moving almost sideways down the hill. Hopefully, he had enough sense to turn and jog at some point. Gus and his friend would have to make a lot of noise to do anything now.

"You okay?" Harper asked the safe-cracker in too soft of a voice as they walked.

"Hurting, but I can make it," Amelia replied quietly also. "Thor has their guns, and all the weight. But he's at least as stubborn as you are."

At the bottom of the slope, the two men stopped. They didn't turn, but didn't move either.

"So we have a problem," Wilkins said.

"No, you don't," Thor called out. "Turn twenty-five degrees to your right and start walking, passing counter-clockwise around that first peak until you're at about one hundred and sixty degrees true. There will be a path that leads up to the access way, along with several false passages designed as traps."

"How do you know that?" Wilkins asked in disbelief, his head turned enough to catch them, but his shoulders stayed put.

"We have a map," Thor said. "With detailed instructions, because nobody knew when we'd be done robbing that train and then crossing the desert. Got passwords and such, too, when we get there."

"Who are you people?" he asked, voice filled with nervous wonder now.

"Matthias Torosyan's gang," Harper spoke up before Thor said anything. "He's dead, but the rest of us made it out and across ahead of the posse that's working on a train wreck back there."

"A train wrecked?" Wilkins did turn now, but that was shock.

"*Postmaster Seventeen*," Thor spoke up. "We were all aboard it when the Scour hit. Winds pulled us right off the tracks, down the slope, then tumbled things into pieces across the valley floor. Took us a couple days to get organized, and we got to cover just as the repair train arrived to take a look at things. Those were the gunshots you heard last night."

"Gunshots?" Wilkins turned to Thor.

Xi had also turned, but Harper was staring right at him, daring him to do something stupid. He looked smarter than that.

"Coyotes or something, back at the camp," Thor said.

"And you have a map," Wilkins stated.

"With all the details we needed to get in, even without the guy that was dealing with your bosses here," Thor assured him. "Faster you all get us there, the sooner we can get out of the sun."

"Okay, I can see that now," Wilkins said. "The Scavenger will still be pissed, but at least he'll be expecting you."

"See, boys?" Harper smiled as they both turned to you. "I told you it would all work out."

CHAPTER 32

He'd been Duff. Now, he was Thor.

Amelia was back to being Red because those names might be known around here. Just as Harper was likely to turn herself back into Lefty, which was kinda a shame, since he was rather liking Harper as a person.

Thor Lonagan. Lefty had whispered it to him as they walked, Red covering the two other men.

He vaguely remembered the two men that the mastermind had sent rearward with Acheson's body, just in time for all three of them to vanish in the storm, apparently forever. Hopefully, somewhere a vulture was getting a good meal of the man Thor was going to impersonate.

And nobody even knew Lonagan's first name, at least according to Lefty. But then, none of the rest had probably known who Harper was.

Thor kept his eyes on the two men up front, watching for them to get stupid, but they seemed resigned. Not like they were leading him and the two women into a trap, but also not like they were going to draw guns and go out in a blaze of glory, either.

Something about knowing which door would be the right one, according the Torosyan's map, did the trick.

They were climbing now, the morning sun beating on their backs and the westerly breeze losing the ability to keep everything cool.

Wilkins led, with Xi behind him on the trail.

Looked like something a wild animal might leave as it went back and forth for water and cover, except that Thor didn't see anything that suggested any sort of water to be had.

Levin had the lake, but most of the rest of the cities just drilled down into the depths to drink. And hit oil when you went deep enough, which was how any of them had survived, since you couldn't trust most metals in the modern age.

"I think this is the right one," Lefty called out, holding the map in one hand and a pistol in the other. "Wilkins?"

"You think or you know?" he called back, glancing over a shoulder.

Thor could see a grin on his face.

"Tell you what," Thor said. "How about you walk in there and open the door?"

He lowered the rifle from his shoulder now, centering on the man.

"That way, if it is a trap, you're the only one who dies," Thor continued. "Or you could suggest a better one and nobody but us will ever know."

Long, ugly pause while a man tried to weigh the value of his life against his honor, when the two were suddenly at odds. The map mentioned death pits and other nasty things.

"Oh, and Xi? You're up next, if you'd like to contribute anything meaningful to the conversation."

The other man gulped audibly.

The two looked at each other and the ghost of a nod passed between them.

Thor drew back the hammer. So did Lefty.

"No, it's okay," Wilkins said. "We walked past the right one, but you'd have to know that to be sure, and passwords at the watchpoint were supposed to verify that you were who you said you were."

"Nobody asked," Harper interjected. "The password was Colorado, if that makes you feel better."

"It does," Wilkins nodded and pointed past them. "We'll walk that way and down a little to the right door and they'll let us in."

"Easy as pie," Thor said, still ready to blast the man backwards on the rocks to bleed his life out.

Lefty reminded him of the way a cat plays with a mouse for a bit before killing it, but Thor was more in tune with stories of a pack of wolves about to tear an antelope apart and eat it.

Wilkins moved slowly, Xi in his wake.

Sure enough, there had been the faintest stutter of a side trail when they got closer. The sort of thing you'd miss if you didn't know, because the dirt and dust shifted as someone stepped onto raw stone instead.

"Xi, you stand over here with me," Red—she was being *Red*, again—ordered the second man. "Wilkins, you and Lefty can go knock."

Thor watched, but he didn't see anything that needed shooting. In a pinch, he'd rely on Red for direction, assuming the first thing she did was kill Xi and then need to reload.

Still, the women seemed to know what they were doing. He could do a pretty good impression of that dumb mook that had been with the women before. Wasn't even all that far off, all things considered.

He certainly wasn't any sort of mastermind, like Torosyan had apparently been.

Right up to the point where it had gotten him killed.

He waited. Muffled sounds from the gap didn't sound like a struggle, let alone gunfire. A long pause ensued.

A man finally stepped out from the gap. Dressed nice in a gray jacket and slacks done in the old, classical style. Medium height and lean in a way that suggested he was taller than he was, when he was maybe shorter than Lefty.

Bald, reddish-brown skull and brown eyes suggested a southern heritage of some sort.

"I see," he said, looking around at Red and Thor.

Lefty and Wilkins emerged a moment later, both looking suitable abashed.

Thor didn't know what the new man saw, but he also didn't have a weapon pointed at the man. That sounded like an even dumber idea now that he'd seen him.

Red got studied closer, but she looked more dangerous.

"Yes, I've heard about you," he nodded, then looked this direction. "And you, Lonagan. It is a shame about Torosyan, but the Scour is an unforgiving mistress. I understand you came into possession of two extra pistols."

"Yes, sir," Thor said, slipping the rifle onto his back by the strap and shifting the bag around to where he could reach into the side pockets.

Two pistols came out and got presented butt-first to the stranger.

"Wilkins, you and Xi return these to Barnett," he said. "Then have them return during the hottest part of the afternoon. Am I clear?"

"Yes, sir," Wilkins said, stepping close to take charge.

They headed back down the hill quickly, leaving the man alone.

Red holstered her pistol. Thor just played big and dumb.

"Lefty tells me that you used to be a lineman once," the stranger said, stepping close to Thor. "And that there is a postal train lying dead across the valley from us."

"Yes, sir," Thor nodded politely. "The crew weren't able to deploy the emergency anchors before the Scour hit us full broadside. It was one of the worst ones I've ever heard of, let alone experienced. Everyone else got killed in the storm. Just vanished, some of them."

"You've been out in a Scour?" he blinked, shock registering in eyes that had been coolly superior until now.

"Small ones, yes," Thor agreed. "The kind that won't carry away a well-set tent, loud as they howl in your head."

"Interesting," he said, sounding more like he was talking to himself.

The man turned and started to head back underground.

"Sir?" Thor called politely. "What name should I call you by?"

The stranger turned and studied him.

Measuring him for a coffin, his mother would have said, but it didn't feel personal.

"Ozolinsh," he replied. "Come."

He walked back into darkness, utterly secure that the three of them would follow.

But what else did Thor have to do?

CHAPTER 33

Red had heard legends about Ozolinsh, but never actually met the man. But then, she'd never needed to go beyond the Nine Cities to flee. By the time she knew that she should have, she'd already been in jail, so it hadn't been an option.

She followed Lefty into the underground darkness, with Thor following her.

It was a tunnel, concealed behind a rock by the way the stone kinked and kind of turned sideways. There was a door that looked like a hunk of stone that had been carved off and polished, then set on pins to rotate. The big crossbar could hold it against anything except the sorts of explosives nobody but her should ever be playing with anyway.

Four men watched them enter, all heavily armed.

Ozolinsh turned once they were all in a large chamber and studied them again.

"Leave your weapons and equipment here," he commanded them in a light voice.

Not playful like a cat. Not angry.

More like a bureaucrat checking off things on a list.

Lefty was already untying cords. Thor put down his bag

and carefully slid the rifle off his shoulder and handed it to one of the men.

Her own gunbelt just unbuckled and got passed off, followed quickly by the other two.

The walls had a set of lockers carved into them, complete with doors. Everything went in, including both gear bags, a padlock was set, and the key was handed into Lefty's custody.

That made Red feel better. She could pick the lock in about two seconds, but Ozolinsh was acting like they'd be getting their gear back at some point.

Might still aim guns at them and open fire right now, and there'd be nothing any of them could do, but they also brought news of the outside world.

Plus, she and Lefty had been sneaky enough to disarm a pair of guards who were probably going to get their asses chewed later.

Ozolinsh nodded when everything was sorted out.

"Follow me," he said simply, stepping to his right into what turned out to be an elevator car.

Probably the one that had summoned him to the surface when Lefty and Wilkins had first knocked.

He smelled clean when they got in and the man closed the door. The other three of them smelled like several days without a shower in dirty clothes, crossing the desert and sweating.

Ozolinsh wasn't wearing any particular scent, but that still marked him as much more civilized than some of the people she'd known in this business.

They rode down in silence.

Red found it a true measure of the man's confidence and power that he didn't bring any guards with him. And any of them could have easily concealed a weapon of some sort, but what good would it do? They were going to be deep under a mountain, trapped until somebody decided to let them out.

And where would they go if they did leave?

Back to jail and the incinerator?

The ride took a while. Ozolinsh was taking them deep into the roots of the mountain. At places like Levin, that was where the poorest of the poor people lived, close to the mechanical equipment and smells. There, the SkyFolk had domes overhead that could protect them from Scours and wind. Whole canyons covered over to grow expensive grains and livestock, supplementing the hydroponics factories and barns where feed animals were raised.

Red wondered if the world of Brigadoon was upside down, with the important people deep. But why would you want to be there?

Obviously, you didn't want domes or anything announcing a hidden city of thieves trying to hide, but what would you find in the depths that would justify the boss living down here?

Except that...

One of the guards had called the leader the Scavenger. Was there something buried down here that they were in the process of digging out?

The ride finally ended with a ding and the door opened. Looking at the controls, Red realized that this was as deep as this elevator went.

Was it the very bottom? Or were there other lifts to take you even further?

The air smelled funny when the door opened. It took her a moment to place.

Moisture. Not just humidity, but actual water vapor in the air. It was chilly down here, too.

Most mountains, you got to a specific temperature once you got below a certain depth, and it never varied from there.

This air was cool enough that she was glad she had her jacket on.

Ozolinsh emerged and began walking. The three of them fell in behind him.

There was no place else to go.

The tunnel was wide, with a strip of overhead lighting that kept things bright. She wondered if there were solar panels of some sort up on top of the mountain, or some sort of Stirling engine running a generator on temperature differentials.

What ancient magic did the Scavenger have access to?

The stone around her was dark. Tool marks showed where it had been carved with metal at some point, so Red wondered if these were ancient tunnels, from before the Scour.

They passed through three sets of doors, each with a pair of guards on them.

She wondered if the Scavenger was in that much danger of being overthrown by other criminals, or just paranoid.

She'd find out shortly.

They entered a larger room. Ceilings vaulted nearly six meters overhead, when most tunnels were barely two and a half. Rough-polished floors and walls were black.

She could see her breath in the air.

On the left, a pool of water. No, an underground stream. Red could see motion as it flowed.

At the center, a platform up a few steps, with a chair she could only classify as a throne, carved out of some stone that shown blood red under the lights in here.

"Wait here," Ozolinsh said, nodding to another pair of armed men and stepping past them to climb the platform and then disappear down a hidden set of steps behind it.

Red was on the right. Lefty on the left. Thor was protected between them.

Sudden light behind the throne suggested a door opening, and then closing.

They waited.

A minute later, the light returned, followed quickly by Ozolinsh and a second figure.

Red presumed male, but there was no way to tell.

He wore dark blue cloth, with heavy boots and what looked like brass kneepads over his pants. Similar brass plates protected his shoulders, with normal looking elbowpads and an equipment belt larger than her normal one, but not that weird.

The weird part was the head.

Or lack of one.

The Scavenger wore an oversized, brass-looking helmet that fully enclosed his skull, with a round, glass window at the front, and smaller ones on his forehead and where his ears would be.

Red supposed that he could see by turning his head inside the massive helmet, because it rested on his shoulders squarely.

Light emerged from the inside of the helmet. No, looking closer it was a ring of lights around the outside of each of the round windows into the helmet.

Definitely weird.

The Scavenger took his place on that big throne and studied them for a long moment.

"Who comes?" he asked in a voice distorted by an electronic amplification system that made him sound almost machine.

"We are part of Matthias Torosyan's gang," Lefty called back carefully. "He was killed in a Scour, along with others, but we have his map and instructions, so we were able to proceed. I am Lefty Solak. This is Red Zhu and Thor Lonagan."

Red listened to the sounds of water dripping somewhere. The space was that silent, and the noise was so strange it kept Red's attention almost focused sideways.

"Torosyan is dead?" the Scavenger asked.

"Correct," Lefty said. "The Scour picked up the train we were robbing and carried it down the tracks and partway across the valley, not that far from Atoll."

"Where is the gold I was promised for safe passage?" the Scavenger asked.

Red had no idea what sort of a deal Matthias had cut with this creature, but obviously something was going on. The problem was that Lefty probably didn't know, either.

Had they come this far, just to blow it at the last lock?

"We have a little gold we were able to salvage," Thor suddenly spoke up.

Red watched him take enough of a step forward that the guards perked up, but he saw it too and stopped.

"In addition, there is an entire postal train that can be salvaged," Thor said.

"My guards tell me that there is a rescue train there, even as we speak," the Scavenger's voice boomed back, like he had turned the amplification up a click. "There will be no salvage."

"That is a repair train, sir," Thor said. "I know. I used to do things like that. They could fix a derail when they repaired the bed and the rails, but the engine of *Postmaster Seventeen* was tumbled and carried more than three hundred meters down the side of the hill. The other five cars went further. Some of them are broken, some not."

"And the linemen won't take them?"

"It would take a thousand men the better part of six

months, just to run a new rail bed down to the wreck," Thor countered. "Then they would need to bring in some sort of heavy equipment to right the engine alone and rerail it. The other cars would take at least as long, but they are just four cargo cars and a crew car. Plus, all have been tumbled and rolled, so most of the plastics and polymers inside would be cracked and crazed. You'd end up having to melt it all down and recast it, just to be safe."

"Then why do I care?" the Scavenger's voice took on an ugly enough tone that Red wished she really did had a spare pistol handy.

It didn't help that Ozolinsh was just standing off to one side, like he had done all he was doing.

"Because the crew compartment still had power to the stove and refrigerator when we left," Thor called back. "So the batteries are intact and can be salvaged. Plus, you can slowly work to strip the rest of the train, but you must do it slowly."

"Why?"

Such a stark, ugly question.

Everyone heard the menace under the words. The guards seemed ready to open fire.

"Because you're a ghost," Thor laughed wickedly. "The monster mothers tell their children about to get them to behave. The linemen will walk around for a few days and inspect the damage. And they'll know someone survived, because we left hints, not cleaning everything up. Since they didn't see us as they came from the south, they might assume we went north, and will probably have already headed that way to try to rescue us by now. But we'll never been seen again, so they'll assume we wandered into the desert and died."

"So?"

"So once they fix the main tracks, the postal trains will start running again," Thor countered as Red studied the guards.

They seemed to be relaxing.

"Every day, at least two trains will go by," Thor continued. "Plus the occasional passenger train like *City of Angels*. And for months, they will look at the wrecks as they transit. If anyone is salvaging the wrecks, or just standing around, they'll be seen. Reported. More people will come from the Nine Cities. Maybe railroad cops, since someone might tell them how close to Atoll you really are. That means trouble."

"But you have a plan," The Scavenger replied.

Red seemed to hear some emotion in those words, however washed out they were. Like the Scavenger was interested. He even looked like he had leaned forward a little, paying attention.

"I was a lineman for a long time, sir," Thor said. "I know what they'll do. How they'll think."

"And?"

"And they'll spend a week inspecting the cars and the rails, because the Scour was the nastiest one I've ever heard of. Worse than any I've been out in," Thor replied. "After that, though, you can start slowly picking up scrap parts and hollowing out the engine and the crew car. There are even books that I doubt the linemen will take. The engineer was a reader. My kind usually aren't."

"What else will we find?" the Scavenger was absolutely engaged now.

Red relaxed some, letting Thor carry things. The man had charisma, when he wanted to use it. Or you got him onto a topic he knew.

She also liked that Thor didn't try to bluff you. If he didn't know something, he didn't lie about it.

He knew rails and engines, in spite of only being a fireman on his first day.

"The crew car was pretty much intact, just too far away from working rails to recover, unless it was critically important. And the shell would have to be stripped anyway, as damaged as it was," Thor said. "Same, the engine will have batteries and generators that can be pulled out and salvaged for use here if nobody notices the thing being emptied. None of the mail cars had anything worth keeping, other than the linemen will grab all the mail that survived so they can deliver it on later."

"And the gold Torosyan promised me?" the Scavenger's voice got hard again.

"We managed to get some of it," Thor lied with a fluid grace that Red found impressive. "Enough that we hoped we'd be able to live here, but not enough to make us all rich. I was hoping you'd hire me and the women on to help salvage the train for you. I know equipment. Red understands electronics. Lefty's really useful when you think about some of the wild animals that might be running around out there on four feet."

"That's your deal?" he boomed down at them.

Thor shrugged. Lefty stepped up now.

"Whatever deal you had with Matthias was lost when the engine tumbled over and he broke his neck," she said. "We don't know any of those details, so we hoped this would be enough."

Red held her breath. Ozolinsh didn't smile, but also wasn't scowling.

The Scavenger was a big, faceless helmet that left you no clue as to what he might be thinking.

"We will consider it," the boss finally said. "Ozolinsh will put you in quarters for now while we send scouts out to study the wreckage and see if it is as you say."

Red let go her held breath slowly and quietly. The chances were that nobody would stumble into the little wash where they'd buried the rest of the gold, because they'd go look closer to the wreck.

What fool would carry fifty kilograms of gold coins by the straps that far anyway, especially in this heat?

She watched Ozolinsh descend from the platform and he even smiled at them, however cold and frosty it was.

"This way," he said simply.

They followed, winding through tunnels and open spaces, but staying on this level.

Eventually, he led them to what looked like an upscale jail. Red had enough experience with them to understand the feel.

Ozolinsh opened a door and gestured for them to precede him. He did follow them in, but only a few steps.

It was an apartment more or less like the one she'd had back in Chesterie, before the most recent time she'd gone to jail. Kitchen and living room, with what looked like a bathroom and four bedrooms off of it. Well-lit and comfortable.

"You'll stay here," Ozolinsh announced with a voice with almost no emotion. "You will be locked in for your own safety, of course. Questions?"

Red had the extra coin from those last ten they'd grabbed. She pulled it out of a pocket now and held it up for the man to see.

It certainly got his attention. The coin itself was more than three centimeters across, and thicker than her fingernail. Shiny new from the mint, also.

"We'd like to apply this to expenses for food and lodging," Red said in the sort of voice she'd use with an innkeeper.

Close enough, anyway.

The coin was stamped with Levin Industrial Treasury on one side and a train engine coming towards you on the other.

Ozolinsh perked right up as he took it from her. If nothing else, it proved that they did have some gold that they had managed to steal. The man might decide to have them strip searched, but it wouldn't get him the rest of the horde, and Red doubted that the others would tell him unless they were being tortured.

At the same time, it marked them as more than your common criminal. That was all she could hope for.

"So noted," Ozolinsh nodded with a warmer smile and Red figured that she'd won them another round.

If they could get the Scavenger on their side, it might all work out.

Or they'd be dead.

CHAPTER 34

Back to Lefty. At least in public.

She was looking forward to just being Harper around Thor. And maybe around Red as well, if they could all find themselves a place here.

She did a quick walk-through of the place, but it was a pretty basic kind of semi-jail.

Thank the gods that Red had been smart enough to bribe Ozolinsh with one of the coins. Based on what Matthias had said, that coin would cover the three of them living a quiet life for as much as half a year, depending. More than enough to get them in the right places.

And maybe they could accidentally find more gold later, and use it to pay better bribes to the Scavenger.

Nobody knew who he was or where he'd come from. The man had been here longer than anybody else, which meant that he was either ancient, or a robot.

The alternative she didn't want to think about was that there might have been several people down the years wearing that suit.

How long ago had Brigadoon started?

Were there really that many people engaged?

She didn't think anybody would know. Those that did wouldn't talk.

Most of the sorts of folks that would end up in a place like this really were common criminals, on the run from the law and lucky enough to make it this far.

Usually by following someone like Matthias into exile, like she'd done.

The three of them ended up back in the main room, sitting around two couches and looking at each other, somewhat at a loss.

Lefty did look over and there were books on a bookcase on a far wall, so at least she'd be entertained for a few days. Thor looked like he'd need some time to recover from everything before she properly seduced him into one of the bedrooms for a good romp.

"What happens next?" Red asked quietly, breaking the spell of silence.

"Maybe a shower," Thor suggested. "They've got water and I'm stinky."

"Me, next," Red said.

Lefty figured she could go last. And maybe walk around mostly naked again until Thor caught a clue and decided to steal a kiss. Or three.

"Will they go for it?" Thor asked, looking directly at her.

She blinked, then stepped past her silly fantasies and back to the present tense. They weren't free yet.

"They have, so far," she replied. "Thanks, Red, for thinking fast. That got his attention."

"Figured it would," Red nodded. "Makes us big-time players instead of mutts that just sidled up to the side door for a scrap."

"I get the feeling you two have done this before," Thor offered, glancing at both of them.

"Something like that," Lefty said. "There's a protocol in crime. A hierarchy of players and favors. Doing things right tells others that you know how the game is played."

"I got a lot to learn," he mused, still lost from the poor, honest lineman he really was.

Would Thor be able to turn himself into a criminal? Lefty hoped so. Harper had uses for the man.

Someone knocked at the main door, and then opened it a moment later. Several men stepped into the room, all of them armed, but nobody pointing guns. And they had all the various bags with them.

"Boss told us to bring these," the first man said, setting her mailbag down on the floor. "All the guns and ammunition are in a box for now, but he said you could have the rest."

Lefty perked up as her satchel, Red's backpack and Thor's long satchel got delivered. The men left and locked the door, but she now had all her gold within sight, assuming nobody had stolen it.

She rose, followed quickly by the others as they each grabbed a bag and started checking.

Yes, the other half of her gold was there. Seven coins, to go with the six she'd stashed in her bra and boots. Serious wealth.

Ozolinsh had to know it was there. Or could have guessed. Hopefully, this was a good sign. Taking them serious at a high-level of play.

Not just another bunch of losers like Barnett and Gus, out there keeping watch badly enough that they could get snuck up on and disarmed.

Lefty grabbed her bag and carried it to the bedroom she was claiming. She'd let Thor sleep alone tonight, assuming Red didn't have needs. And there wasn't much in the way of clothing she'd managed to pack. Most of everything had vanished with Pedro and the other Lonagan, after her assumption that once she got here, she'd be able to buy more or hire a tailor.

Supposedly, the population of Brigadoon was at least a third female, but she'd seen only one woman in the hallways they crossed, and one as a guard on one of the doors. Still, there ought to be clothing she could buy.

Not like she could sew worth a damn, but she'd never intended to be the least bit domestic. She'd have servants for that sort of thing if they pulled this off.

Lefty emerged at the same time as Red, what little she owned packed. Thor had barely any more personal gear, so she stuck her head into his bedroom and watched him organizing things on a shelf with the sort of meticulous care that surprised her.

But then, he was a careful man. She knew that.

He had removed his longcoat and laid it over a chair, but kept the rest of his gear on. At least for now. As had she.

Someone knocked again, but Red was out there and could deal with them.

"Lefty," Red called a moment later.

She stepped out as Thor looked up at her and blushed, apparently lost in his own world.

A man stood there in the door. Better dressed than a goon, but not as well done as Ozolinsh had been.

"I'm here for the male," he announced sharply. "The Scavenger had other questions."

"We're a team," Red countered in an equally testy voice.

"Noted," the man nodded to her. "But it wasn't a question. I'm to retrieve him alone. Food will be delivered for the two of you shortly."

Thor emerged now, looking a little lost.

Things were moving, but Lefty felt like it had just slipped out of her hands and was about to fall down a drain to be lost forever.

Thor looked at everyone for a long moment then squared his shoulders like a man walking to his execution.

Red caught her eye and the look that woman gave her promised mayhem, so Lefty felt better.

The door closed behind him and Lefty growled to herself.

"Hopefully, this is good news," Red offered, but Lefty wasn't mollified.

Felt like someone was splitting them up to play a game of Prisoner's Dilemma.

Isolate everyone and keep track of the lies, so you can trip them up later.

The game had just gotten sharp.

CHAPTER 35

Thor followed the man through a variety of tunnels that probably were meant to confuse most people. He just paid attention and counted doors and turns as he went.

Eventually, he ended up at a double door that was locked. The man he was following knocked and someone opened it from the inside.

"In you go," the stranger said, not following, and Thor found himself stepping through into a living room not all that different from the one he'd just left. A suite, maybe, about five meters across and ten or so long, with four meter ceilings instead of the lower ones everywhere else. Good lighting for underground. The furniture was nicer, with two couches at a square angle and a chair.

"Please, be seated," a voice behind him said, and Thor remembered that someone had opened the door unseen.

He turned and studied her.

Tall for a woman, even talker than Harper. Muscular in the way of someone that does physical labor, rather than one of the SkyFolk who have gymnasiums they can visit in between business meetings.

Brownish hair had been cut as short as his, but she didn't have the sorts of tan and leathery skin you got from being out in the sun on a line gang.

Not homely, but not beautiful ether. Dressed simply, in slacks and a tucked in shirt, both gray in complementary shades.

She gestured with one hand and Thor took the better part of valor, ending up on the near couch. They were soft to sit on, and he hoped that he wasn't doing any damage with the armor plates on the outside of his pants or vest.

The woman sat on the other couch, turned sideways with a leg tucked under her and an arm across the back to study him, looking far more relaxed with the situation than Thor felt.

He was back to dealing with SkyFolk, secure in their power and wealth, and he was just a mutt in from the sun.

"I heard what you told the Scavenger," she began in a pleasant, alto voice. "How much of the train can be salvaged?"

Thor paused and tried to put it into words so he wasn't hemming and hawing about as he spoke.

"The crew car continued to have power right up until the moment we left," he replied. "The refrigerator still worked, as did the stove. I didn't try to do anything with the engine itself, so I don't know, but it had power for the emergency lights at least."

"But you think someone will see if we started stripping it?" she said, pursuing the same logic as the Scavenger had earlier.

"I think they'll notice people," Thor said. "If we were careful to stay inside the shells, and only move around after dark, then it might be a while before anyone realized something was happening. If then. They might just assume that it was breaking down under the heat."

"How much polymer is there?" she asked, eyes blazing with intensity.

Thor wondered if they didn't have a well here for tapping the deep oil. He'd seen water flowing in the main room, and there was a lot of spare metal around down here, but access to plastic in the Age of the Scour had been one of the reasons the Nine Cities had been able to thrive and rebuild.

You couldn't trust iron.

"A bunch," he answered. "If you strip the four mail cars from the inside, you should get tons. Or you could slowly bury one to hide it."

"You said they would notice," she leaned forward a little.

"If you did it a little at a time, they might assume that it was wind pushing drifts," he said. "I was thinking years of work, so you snuck everything out from under them."

"Are you capable of that kind of work?" she asked in a hard, cold voice.

"I was a Senior Lineman before I became a criminal," Thor said. It was even true, as long as the timing wasn't checked up on too closely. "I understand working in the heat and the sun with a gang to get things done. Most of that equipment would just be scrapped and melted down again anyway if they got it back to Levin, so they aren't losing anything by leaving it here."

"And your friends?" she pivoted the conversation in a way that had Thor feeling vertigo, so he fell back on truths they had told him were safe.

"Lefty is a gunslinger," he said. "First time I met the woman she was looking over her pistols at me, but we get along fine today. Red's a safecracker and lockpicker who can open damned near anything. Plus, she understands electronics, which will help if the salvage still has live power somewhere.

The panels on the roof might work, but I didn't check, since we weren't staying."

She leaned back now and studied him.

As much brains as his two partners, if he had to guess.

"What were you planning to do with the gold you did have?" she pivoted again.

"Retire," he said. "Been working my whole life for a pension that's never coming now. Got more money than I know what to do with, but still trying to figure out what I want out of this world, you understand?"

She nodded silently but offered no opinion.

"Thought about using it to maybe fund some explorations," Thor let his guard down a little. "See if anyone survived east of the desert, or maybe in the far north."

"The rails don't run there," she noted.

"Understood," Thor nodded. "But we used to be able to fly, before the Scour. Maybe that's possible again. Or we could build ground trains that don't require tracks, so we can travel to the old places and see what survived. A man who just settles into a chair to watches vids for the rest of his life won't end up living long, so I figure I need something to get me out of bed tomorrow. And all the other tomorrows. Impossible dreams are the best for that sort of thing."

"Indeed?" she seemed to relax. "Are you an impossible dreamer, Thor Lonagan?"

"Maybe," he shrugged, considering it. "But I'm also a technician and a lineman, so it has to be the practical dreams, and not silly love poetry by folks who never got their hands dirty or bled on a piece of equipment they were trying to fix."

It dawned on him that he'd never been introduced to this woman. Just dropped headlong into a conversation. She was important folks, that much was obvious. And there was only the two of them in here, but he supposed she could yell for help and someone would come along and shoot him.

Nobody was dumb enough to meet with a big, strong stranger like him without doing something to tilt the scales their way.

Asking her right out though sounded rude. Felt rude.

Whole situation felt weird, but he wasn't used to sitting in pretty salons talking to smart women, either.

Thor fell back on silence as a meaningful weapon, just studying the woman. Thorstein had done that a lot, when he was breaking new gandy dancers to his will.

Just stare at them with them hard eyes.

Hers were green of a sort. Lighter than brown, but not that sharpness of Harper's.

Didn't miss anything, though. That much was clear.

A smile crept into them finally, after he was pretty sure she was going to have him thrown out on his ear.

"So you're the kind that dreams of better machines, Thor Lonagan?" she asked, again using his name as a weapon.

He could either take it, or break down and ask hers.

That felt like showing the wrong kind of weakness. At least today.

"That's right," he countered with a fierce shrug. "World was a better place, once. Ought to be a way to get it back. I got decades before I'm too old to do something about it."

"And your friends?" she asked.

More whiplash.

"Partners," he said. "Only way we were getting out of that train and to here was as a team. Keeping it that way."

She studied him some more. Kinda like Lefty did, but not as nice about it.

"Just partners?" she asked, those eyes getting sharp and cold again. "Nothing more?"

Oh.

Well, crap.

Now she had that same look in her eyes that Lefty had, strutting out of the bathroom damned near naked and smiling at him.

No good way to answer that question. Or any of them that might follow.

And he didn't feel like lying now, after getting this far on the truth.

"Haven't been with any woman in maybe six months," he said flatly, emphasizing *any* and challenging her to say anything more. "Never been married, either. Man like me's never home enough."

He figured to leave out the drunk and rowdy bits. Anybody who didn't know linemen home after a week on the desert, coin rich and ready for a good bender, didn't understand how his business worked.

He was usually sober enough to not get into any fights. Well, maybe not start any. That was close enough.

Size mattered when folks got upset. They could meander off to another bar if they felt that insulted. Or get thumped.

The woman studied his face. Seemed to be reading his soul, but there wasn't much complicated on the topic.

"We'll talk again, Thor Lonagan," she announced, unfolding graceful enough and standing.

Sounded like a dismissal, so Thor shot out of that sofa and turned his head right to the door.

She hadn't moved much when he got there and looked back, one hand on the handle.

Cryptic face.

Thor couldn't tell if he'd passed whatever test she had for him or failed, but he'd been him, and that was about as good as it got.

"How long will you be here, Thor?" she asked in a quieter voice.

"Long as the Scavenger and the others got a use for me, ma'am," he smiled grimly. "Strong back and lineman skills I can always fall back on. Hopefully more."

"Hopefully," she nodded cryptically.

One hand gestured for him to go. It wasn't a dismissal so much as a goodbye-for-now sort of wave.

Still, he took his cue and pulled the door open.

Two men on the other side, damned surprise when he joined them and pulled it shut behind him.

"Someone want to escort me back to my place?" he asked.

"Dunno where you came from," the one on the left said.

"That's okay," Thor nodded. "I know the way."

That one fell into step beside him after a few strides anyway, but didn't say anything as Thor retraced his steps and counts.

Brigadoon was going to be even more complicated than he'd imagined.

CHAPTER 36

The whole idea of showers interrupted, Red watched Lefty get a little twitchy, and then head back into her room and grab the book she'd stolen from the train. Red recognized the cover, but didn't ask.

Instead, she dug out a couple of practice locks from her kit and worked on opening them. They sat in silence and waited.

Pretty quickly, the door opened and two plates of food got delivered by a well-dressed waiter with a rolling cart who departed after leaving them a full pitcher of clean water and some kind of stew with cornbread on the side.

Or a good approximation of cornbread.

The two of them moved to the table in one corner and settled for a meal.

Red wondered if they had good hydroponics factories here, since there seemed to be enough water, or had traded with one of the cities under the table.

Red had never done the black market side of things to know. She was the one folks hired to steal something for someone else. Hand it off and get paid. Go steal the next thing.

Felt like maybe she should pay a little better attention to

the whole food chain now. Learn the business of crime. Lefty was a gunslinger, and Thor was too honest for his own good, at least until the two of them sanded some of that off the man and turned him into one of them.

Could she and Lefty turn him into another Matthias? A nicer version that took care of his people, and wasn't such an asshole most of the time?

They ate. The tension wasn't anything personal. Thor wasn't here, and that was a bad sign, more times than not.

Lefty might have some personal feelings there, but Red was always more self-contained that way.

So she smiled at the woman and made small talk. Too much unknown, and too much risk of the walls having ears, so nothing important could be discussed.

"How heavy was that safe on the last car?" Lefty finally asked out of the blue as they were eating.

"Maybe thirty-five kilos," Red guessed. "That's what the civilian version of that model weighs, anyway, and I didn't see anything about it that would change it much. You were supposed to bolt those things to the floor, like someone does in their home, but I'm guessing they figured the weight of coin would hold it for long enough to get down to Jacumba. Why?"

"Seemed to be in pretty good shape," Lefty said. "Would the locks be okay?"

"Perfectly fine, except where some grit might get into the tumblers by now," Red replied, letting the woman draw the conversation out. "Five minutes with some oil and you'd think it was new from the manufacturer. Thinking about bringing it here?"

"Going to be worth money to the Scavenger, I presume," Lefty nodded. "And light enough to move easy. Maybe get a cart, or would that leave tracks?"

"I'd think tracks," Red said. "Need to ask Thor when he gets back. Maybe four big guys just grab corners and haul it out of sight to a wagon of some sort. Not sure how you hide things in the desert. Probably all set to learn, though, if they want to pick Thor's brain on things like that."

"You suppose that's what's happening?" Lefty asked in a leading way.

"Don't have any better idea," Red replied, letting that one slide without committing.

She started to say more, but the door suddenly opened and Thor walked it. He turned to someone outside.

"They're eating," he said. "Can you ask if someone will bring me some?"

"Sure," a man said before the door closed again.

Both women rose and studied him, but he smiled and plopped down in one of the open chairs.

"I'd steal some cornbread, but maybe they'll have some for me," he said in a tired voice.

"Everything okay?" Red asked, watching his body language.

Embarrassment to some degree, with a little bit of anger twisted sideways.

Not sure who it was aimed at, but not her or Lefty.

"Got interviewed by some woman in charge," Thor said in a calculatedly-offhand way that didn't sound anywhere as inno-cent as the words. "She wanted to know what I knew about the wreck and how to salvage it. Got the feeling she's going to tell the Scavenger one way or the other what to do with us."

Red watched the flash of fire that vanished out of Lefty's eyes almost as fast as it appeared.

"Also told her we were a team," Thor volunteered. "A package deal for such a salvage job. And anything else."

Ah ha. So she hadn't been some ancient hag of a woman, but maybe somebody that Lefty would get a little jealous about.

Red kept her smile to herself. That was another one of the reasons she didn't bother getting attached to any of the men who had wandered along and made her various offers over the years.

"And then?" Lefty managed, sounding almost calm and rational.

Almost.

"And then she dismissed me and I came back here," Thor replied, turning to look square at Lefty. "Now we see if they hire the three of us to work the wreck."

She had to give the man credit. He understood, at least at an unconscious level, that there were emotions going on here that might cause some trouble later. Lefty wasn't the kind of woman who could survive by herself in a quiet, empty room, but would start climbing the walls and banging on the door after a while as the crazy built up.

Thor was more like Red, but she supposed that a lineman had to work by himself at times, with just his own thoughts to keep him company.

Had one of the Scavenger's aides decided to take a closer look at the big newcomer? Likely.

Most of the men Red had seen inside these walls, and the four outside, weren't any of them as big as Thor across the shoulders. Some of them might be smarter, but the man had been successful at his career, right up to the point his honesty got him into trouble with someone.

The kind of trouble that got them all here.

"So that's it?" Lefty asked in exactly the offhand tone Thor had used earlier.

had used earlier.

"Hopefully, someone brings me some food," he smiled. "Then we wait until they decide what to do with us."

Red watched Lefty relax. The woman's shoulders came down from around her ears. The scowl lines in her forehead softened and vanished.

They finished their food about the time the waiter returned with his rolling cart and more grub.

Someone had thoughtfully included desert this time. Looked like little sweet cakes, the kind you made with boiled beets and fresh carrots.

Thor ate in relative silence, probably unaware that they had delivered him more than twice as much food as either she or Lefty had gotten.

Red watched Lefty's anger go back up a notch, but didn't say anything.

She didn't know. None of them did. Might just be that the woman had decided that Thor was someone she wanted to hire and was being nice. And wasn't just making a subtle play at Thor right now, to see how the two women might react.

Red would smile. Lefty would, too, but it would be a false kind of smile.

Hollow and brittle.

Red wondered if Thor was utterly doomed at this point, trapped between the two women, neither of whom had any real claim on him.

She also wondered if either of them realized how stubborn the man really could be when pushed. She'd seen it in his eyes at times when Lefty wasn't necessarily paying attention.

Tough, but capable of getting downright mean if threatened. However, he could also go the other way. Red had vague, out-of-focus memories of the man fixing her cracked rib.

That had involved stripping her topless and touching her, but she didn't remember him taking any liberties, then or later.

And Lefty was pretty adamant that all the two of them had done that second night was cuddle, fully dressed. And she wasn't one to lie, so Red would take that at face value.

She also knew that Thor was replacing Matthias in Lefty's mind, if not yet her bed, providing the woman impetus to do things. Dreams, since she really didn't seem to have any of her own.

Red had dreams, but most of them had simply revolved around escaping all the various warrants and jailers long enough to run away forever. Like Thor, she needed to find something bigger, if they really had reached that brass ring moment and managed to pull it off.

Maybe she needed to seduce Lefty tonight and let Thor have his sleep? It was a two-birds, one-stone kind of solution, but she figured she'd save it for later, if things got a little more awkward than they were now. And her ribs were still a little sore.

Thor seemed to understand how fragile things around him were. His eyes gave him away when she caught him glancing this way.

"Partners," she said aloud, as if out of the blue, rather than at the far end of a lot of logic.

Nobody knew what was happening next.

Even Matthias hadn't had anything better than getting as far as Brigadoon, and then having enough money to buy his way in and live a life of debauchery. But he was like that.

Red had never participated in any of his offers and romps. She didn't need that crap inside a team.

Hopefully, Lefty would catch a clue on that front. If

someone on the inside here thought Thor was cute, maybe they could leverage that to their advantage.

243

CHAPTER 37

Lefty had actually managed to lose herself in the book after breakfast. Lunch. Whatever it was.

The clock in the suite said early afternoon, but when you lived underground, that didn't mean much. People came and went according to whatever the clock said, rather than the sun, because most people never saw the sky.

Thor had taken a shower and changed into those silly pants and the nice shirt, which made him look like a railroad engineer instead of a lineman. He had pulled a book off the shelf and was reading it on the other couch.

Red was taking her turn getting clean now, leaving the two of them alone.

Lefty caught him looking at her over the top of his book.

Like she was already looking at him.

Glancing around, she wondered if there were microphones and cameras recording everything they did, to see if they were spies.

Can't be too careful, especially when you're outlaws, but Lefty wasn't sure what those fine folks of the Nine Cities might do about the place.

Would they wipe it out?

Somebody, somewhere, had to know that Brigadoon actually existed. And had contacts in the cities, since Matthias hadn't been here, but communicated with them well enough that he had been expected.

How convoluted were things? How deep did the conspiracies go?

She'd only ever been a killer, not a thinker. Red could think. Thor could, too. Maybe she needed to stop reacting to everything and actually have a plan?

That frightened her even more, since she'd gone more than a decade not being anything more than a fancy wind-up doll. At least, if she was willing to be truthful with herself.

She'd always turned away from self-reflection, but maybe she needed to face that mirror finally?

The time for continued self-delusion had probably passed in that instant when that engine lifted up into the air and Thor had grabbed her, holding her tight so that she didn't end up like Matthias or the boys.

Dead.

Obviously, the gods had a plan for her. That was what all the holy-rollers always said, even when they were completely full of shit.

Maybe she just needed to grow up and admit it.

It didn't help that Red and Thor were in their thirties and she was barely twenty-six. The time for stupid was over.

She closed the book and rose.

Thor's eyes got a little scared as she stepped across and sat down next to him, close enough to touch. He seemed frozen, so she noted his page, closed his book, and set it on the coffee table.

Assuming someone was watching, she wanted to give them

a good show, so she draped herself on his side and put her nose up close to his ear like she was nuzzling it.

"Sit perfectly still," she murmured, feeling him jump just a little. "We need to talk. Or I do and you need to listen. Okay?"

She felt trite. How many times had some woman started a conversation off that way? How many of those ever worked out of the best?

She leaned close and smelled how clean he'd gotten. Kissed him on the cheek, feeling freshly shaven skin against her lips.

"I'm assuming that we're being watched, all the time we're in here," she murmured as she slowly burrowed her way into his arms and maybe his life. Regardless of what he had planned. "We don't know what they're up to. Or what they want from us."

"Yes," breathed as he leaned close enough to kiss her on the ear now. "But we're all outside the law now."

"A week ago, we were all strangers, Thor," she continued in a low voice, letting her hand drift across his chest like this was a proper seduction, and not a performance for the Scavenger and whoever else was watching. "Now we're here and I want us to be a team. A partnership, including Red. Us three against the world. Are you okay with that?"

She realized that she'd only ever assumed the man, instead of asking him, but the past was done.

He turned into her and kissed her on the cheek as well.

"That's the only way I expect we'll all stay alive," he murmured back, one hand coming up to caress her shoulder.

She could feel how tightly wound he was. Probably sat there for the last hour waiting for her to explode in a jealous rage.

And it was all her fault.

A week ago, she probably would have, had Matthias gotten

treated like that when the old group arrived. Two days ago, she'd been dangling herself in front of Thor, just to tease and tempt him, before realizing how different he was from Matthias, and all the rest.

How much better than the common criminals of her past.

"If she demands it, you should take her to bed," Lefty said, nuzzling at his ear. "We need to be safe and secure here as a base. Then we can figure out how to get the rest of the gold and how long we can stay here."

"What about you two?" he asked, twisting further around so that an arm could get around her shoulders.

Somehow, they ended up flat on the couch and tangled up, his weigh pinning her down.

In a good way.

"We won't mind," Lefty admitted quietly, both to him and to herself. "You'll do what you have to do to keep us all safe."

He leaned close and kissed her on the mouth before leaning back a little and smiling.

"I meant if one of you demanded I take them to bed?" he asked in a much less innocent voice. "How should I respond?"

She reached up and pulled him back down to her for another kiss.

"You should definitely not resist such a thing," Lefty said, reaching around those shoulders and feeling the slabs of hard muscle under that shirt as one leg slipped around the back of his thigh. "They probably have a very good reason for it, so you should play along and pretend to enjoy yourself."

He didn't appear to be pretending.

Neither did she.

"So I'm to serve you?" he grinned, leaning down and kissing the side of her neck.

She purred. Matthias would have them both half-naked by now and already grinding between her legs.

Thor hadn't even caressed the outside of her shirt.

"You should," she growled quietly. "Anything I demand."

"Does that involve carrying you into the bedroom?" he asked, one hand finally meandering down her side and around her bottom as they kissed.

"Absolutely," Lefty decided, rubbing herself up against him.

Whoever this other woman might be, at least Lefty would have him first.

Then they'd figure out how to be rich here.

CHAPTER 38

Red tiptoed to her bedroom wrapped in a towel, and slipped in silently.

Thor and Lefty had ended up in his bedroom, but left the door enough ajar that Red could hear what the two of them were up to.

Right now, Lefty was loud enough that the guards outside probably knew what she was up to.

On balance, probably a good thing to relieve that much stress in a good way. Gods below knew both Thor and Lefty needed something like that after the last few days.

She'd been in the shower, getting clean for the first time in a week, so Red didn't know who had worked up the gumption first, but Lefty was getting a good workout. Probably Thor, too.

Red started to close her door when she noticed a package sitting on the coffee table that hadn't been there when she decided she wanted a long shower earlier.

The towel around her was big enough that she didn't show anything off, and Thor and Lefty had both seen most of it already. Plus, they were occupied enough that a bomb might go off out here without them noticing.

Red stepped back into the main room and approached.

Turned out to be a pile of packages. Top one was clothing.

Taking it out and looking at the gray shirt, it would be about her size. Someone who understood clothing had sent this. Underneath, pants that she could roll up, from the way they hung against her leg.

Quickly, Red sorted through everything, leaving the two lovebirds a pair of piles on the couch when they finally emerged for water.

Red went back and got dressed. Black pants. Gray shirt. Her old socks and boots. The bathroom had had a comb and soap, so she felt almost civilized at this point.

Clock said mid-afternoon, getting on towards dinner, so she wondered if the Scavenger would come for them tonight, or wait until the morning. Hopefully, the coin she'd given to Ozolinsh was paying off in good ways. Food. Clothing. Meetings with important people.

Now, they just had to figure out if the Scavenger wanted to deal.

CHAPTER 39

Clean clothes. Clean body. Good romp. Enough sleep.

Thor finally felt relaxed for the first time in so long he couldn't really remember.

Months, maybe.

Since he'd been summoned by the shop bosses who wanted to have a quiet meeting about accusations he'd made. Not in public at the monthly hall meeting, mind you, but in a place where things could be kept hushed up and settled without anyone necessarily going to jail.

That hadn't worked out the way anybody expected.

He was in the main salon of their suite, reading the book that he'd gotten into before being interrupted by Lefty.

She was across from him, also reading, but far more relaxed than she'd been yesterday. Something about getting her back scratched in the shower, maybe.

Red was at the kitchen table, working on one of her locks with her back to the corner so she could see both of them.

There had been chicory coffee earlier, with breakfast, but it was done now.

Now, they waited.

In his head, Thor had just about timed it perfectly, for reasons he couldn't have told anyone. Just knew the instant someone was going to knock on their door, open it, and step in.

Ozolinsh.

Looking calm and relaxed. New day, new solutions.

Maybe new crimes to commit. What did you do when you ran a criminal enterprise hidden in the desert?

Everyone had risen when the man entered the room.

He smiled at them serenely, a man utterly in control of any situation.

"Would you care to join me?" he asked.

As if they'd turn him down.

Thor let the women lead and took up a spot behind them. The new clothing was black pants for everyone. Red had a gray shirt, Lefty blue, and he was in green for now.

And everything fit.

Ozolinsh led them back to the main throne room they'd been in yesterday.

Weren't the same guards, but the same numbers and personality from the look of them.

Ozolinsh left them and went through to the room in back where the Scavenger had been yesterday. Same light from a door opening, then again as he returned.

Scavenger.

Man, that had to be weird, dressed up in what Lefty had finally decided looked like an ancient diving suit, back when it was safe to be in the ocean for any stretch of time. Big helmet that rendered the man unrecognizable. Brass on the corners for protection.

Booming, anonymous voice.

Thor glanced around the big room. There were maybe

twenty people here today, mostly off on the left and standing around. He didn't see the woman who'd interviewed him, but these people had the look of engineers and technicians available to answer questions, rather than the important people he'd seen yesterday.

None of them had that thing that Ozolinsh or the Scavenger gave off.

Power.

The Scavenger took his place on the throne and studied them for a few moments before he spoke. Ozolinsh remained up on the platform, off to one side, standing casually.

"I have spoken with my people," the Scavenger boomed. "They tell me that the job to strip the train of all useful gear and salvage can be done, but must be executed slowly. Carefully, lest we lead the railroad police of the Nine Cities directly to our doorstep, when they do not know where to find us."

He paused. The way the man's voice was amplified was just enough to ripple echoes off the back walls behind Thor, like waves in his beer glass.

The room settled.

Thor had ended up in the middle again, with Red on his right and Lefty on his other side. Felt like the way they would be as a team.

He could work with that.

Everyone waited for the Scavenger.

"Thor Lonagan, you claim to have the skills to perform this task," the Scavenger finally broke the lingering silence.

"That's right," he replied, just loud enough to be heard, but not enough to maybe constitute a threat.

Or a brag. Thorstein had broken him of that sort of thing a long time ago.

"If I put a team at your disposal, what would you need?" the man asked in a better tone, even through the amplification.

Less threatening. More technical, like maybe the one lady had understood everything to her satisfaction and explained it to the boss.

"A wagon or cart to transport pieces quickly across the desert floor, without leaving tracks visible to anyone on a train passing by," Thor answered. "People dressed in sand and dirt colors who might vanish if they had to fall to the ground to hide suddenly as a train came by off schedule. Tools. Technicians who understand salvage and can take orders if I'm in charge. Patience. And a couple of gunslingers to deal with any animals that take exception to us being there. There are at least three dead bodies around the wreck somewhere that might bring cats or wolves down for the carrion."

Thor ran out of words, but he'd already worked out a lot of it in his head, laying there and listening to Lefty purr as he was wrapped around her. He didn't know the names of some of the things he'd need someone to make for him, but he had the images well enough to describe.

The Scavenger just watched. Thor waited.

Finally, the Scavenger turned to the group on the side.

"Stirling Chan," he said ominously.

A short, fairly pudgy man stepped out of the group. He crossed about halfway and came to rest, facing the Scavenger and giving a half-bow that looked formal.

"Will you take orders from this man, Chan?" the Scavenger asked in a stilted tone that just felt weird to Thor.

Chan turned this way now and their eyes met. Stirling Chan had wrinkles around his eyes and smile that seemed to glow about him. They studied each other for a long moment.

"Ozolinsh tells me you were a lineman, in the surface world," Chan said in a flat tone.

"That's right," Thor agreed. "Been in my share of Scours and derails over the years."

"What do you know about battery systems and induction relays?" Chan challenged.

"Not a damned thing," Thor smiled at the man. "In charge means I have experts who know how to disarm things and strong backs to move them onto wagons to be brought back here. It means that I know how to schedule a team and adjust as things move faster or slower than originally anticipated. That I can keep track of folks so that nobody works so hard that they wander off into the desert dog tired and get lost."

Chan's eyes narrowed as Thor spoke, but he didn't seem angry.

"You ever kill anybody, Lonagan?" he asked.

Thor laughed. He pointed both thumbs outward at the pretty ladies he'd come to this party with.

"Don't have to," he told the smaller man. "That's why I have Lefty and Red."

Personally, Thor had no idea if Red had ever killed someone, but if she had the reputation for it, chances were she wouldn't have to start now.

He had no doubts about Lefty.

None whatsoever.

Chan seemed to appreciate that distinction. He nodded to Thor, and then turned back to the Scavenger and bowed again.

"He'll do," Chan said.

The Scavenger seemed to be studying Thor for a long moment. Maybe including the women in that look, but you couldn't see anything going on inside that helmet.

"Thor Lonagan, welcome to the business," he finally said. "Don't do anything to make me regret that decision."

CHAPTER 40

Thor found himself back out on the surface, with Lefty, Red, and Stirling along for the ride. The sun would be going down any moment.

They'd spent two days thinking and planning. Thor had not been surprised to discover more than one secret door into the mountain. This particular entrance was big enough for a cart with pneumatic tires, electric motors, and a flatbed large enough for a pair of coffins side by side.

If Thor had anybody else to bury.

Stirling drove. Turned out the man was a jack of just about any trade you wanted to mention, if you went back far enough. Wanted for murder, arson, robbery, kidnapping, and various other swindles, but generally an agreeable-enough fellow once you got past all that.

The wagon was a frame with a bench seat up front and a flatbed behind that with a tall rollbar to hold onto. Six big wheels with teeth in them dug into the sand and dirt well enough.

Thor had ended up seated next to Chan, with Red and Lefty standing behind them. The cart could get up to nearly sixty kilometers per hour, but Chan wasn't in that great of a hurry. Cutting across the floor on the ancient roads, he figured to get to the wreckage of the train just about the time it got dark enough that you needed lights.

Thor looked, but didn't see the rescue train. Scouts reported that it had departed the morning after it arrived, having left a team of linemen to inspect things. He assumed that the train had gone north looking for him and Acheson, on the assumption that the two of them must had started walking.

He didn't know if the rules and training were to stay with the train in such a disaster, because again he didn't know.

Fireman. Day One.

Eventually, the train had returned and picked up the line crew. Thor assumed that folks would return at some point to maybe do some salvage, but once you grabbed all the mail that had survived, did you really strip the place bare?

Sounded more ghoulish than any team Thor had ever been on, back when he'd been Duff. But he'd never dealt with a train rolled off the tracks, or a crew that had vanished.

At least the tracks themselves looked to be in good shape, both sets. Otherwise, the rescue team might have had to stay put for a few weeks, especially if the Postmaster engine had dragged across the ground and damaged a rail bed in the process.

Was it a good thing, all in all, that the storm had been strong enough to pick a whole train up and carry it across the other set of tracks before tumbling it?

Thor could barely remember anything, once Lefty had fallen out of the sky like an angel and he'd caught her. Tumbling, screaming, banging, howling.

Noise. Then darkness.

Hopefully, a Scour like that was a once-in-a-lifetime kind of storm.

The breeze in his face was nice. Thor was back in his heavy gear, same as the women. Stirling was comfortable in pants and a jacket with no armor, but he also expected to be crawling into things to disconnect them and inspect them. Nobody was stealing anything tonight, so much as doing a better inventory than Thor had done before he set out.

Why would he care about any of that, if he was abandoning it forever? At the time, all he had to look forward to was making it to Brigadoon. That, or dying when the next set of assassins found him.

"How close are we?" Stirling called over the hiss of the sand and dirt on the hard, rubberized tires.

Six of them made a racket.

"Just around the curve here," Thor pointed. "We derailed about five kilometers south of the old ruins at Atoll. Everything went roughly northwest from there. Wreckage field is about a kilometer across."

"Glad I wasn't up in that mess," Stirling whistled.

"Worst storm I've ever even heard of," Thor replied. "Let alone lived through. Most of them are little things that just electrocute you if you have any iron or copper on you that hasn't been insulated properly. This one killed a train."

They came around the curve finally, and there was still just enough light on the floor that Thor heard Stirling see it for the first time.

"Shit," the man said. "That's a train engine?"

"On the left, yes," Thor said, pointing as he spoke. "The crew car where we hid out for a day. Four cargo cars instead of the normal three."

"Okay, let's do the crew car tonight, since you said it still had power," Stirling began to curve the nose of the cart that direction. "That means it's likely in the best shape, anyway."

"What about coyotes and cats?" Lefty called from behind them.

She had Thor's big rifle unslung and in her hands, ready to shoot.

"Not many around here," Stirling said. "I'm guessing some fool heard the howls you mentioned and spooked. Maybe he saw heat waves shimmering in the light and thought it was movement. One idiot fires, the rest tend to cut loose."

Thor nodded. Sounded like something a line team would do. Not that he was proud of that, but when it doubt, always make sure the other guy went down first.

Worked in bar fights, too.

Thor studied the desert floor as Stirling drove. The Scour had stripped it pretty much down to rock and baked soil in passing, and it would take a while for more grit to blow in and leave a soft layer.

On the one hand, that was good, because they wouldn't necessarily leave a trail as they drove. On the other, the wheels would eventually damage the ground enough to make tracks, if they drove around too fast.

Which was why Stirling was approaching the last kilometer or so at a sedate roll barely faster than Thor could have run.

It only took one person seeing something that shouldn't be there, then telling the authorities about it.

What would the SkyFolk of the Nine Cities do when they found out that there were other places people lived, not under their control? Not just Brigadoon, apparently, from something Stirling had hinted at in passing.

Or did they already know, and just not tell the little people?

A whole criminal underworld out there. Not big enough to

take over any of the cities, but not working or trading directly with them, either. At least out in the open.

How much of the truth had remained hidden from the average Joe, working in his dead-end job, like on a line or at an injection molder?

What would people do if they didn't have to live petty lives?

That was the thing he found himself coming back to again and again. Made him angry, too. However, it wasn't anything he needed to worry about today.

Stirling finally pulled up to the back side of the crew car when seen from the tracks. With the sun down, they looked like part of the dark lump that was train wreckage, and the plan was only to be here for a few hours, giving Stirling a chance to understand what him and folks he'd be bringing would need to do.

Thor took a deep breath and climbed out. Lefty was already down and standing guard. Red had mostly healed, but was moving with the care of someone still enjoying the ability to draw a deep breath without wincing. Stirling stood up and reached out a hand to just touch the skin of the car.

The shell was that nifty mix of polymers and metal shavings that didn't conduct electricity in a Scour, but had more strength than just polymer alone. Stronger than even steel, but more brittle. Wouldn't dent, but that was the problem.

The surface showed a crazed pattern of flaws, like Thor had stood off a middle distance and fired at it with a shotgun, every pellet cracking it.

They'd have to break it all down with alcohol and heat and recast it, but there was a tremendous amount of material here to salvage, if you were careful.

"How did it land on its wheels?" Stirling asked.

"Mystery for the ages," Red answered, moving around to the rear of the car.

Thor watched the horizon both directions, but there was nothing to be seen.

"So what're your thoughts on this, Thor?" Stirling asked as everyone followed the safe-cracker.

"If it can be repaired, this makes a really good base from which we might operate," he replied. "Assuming nobody else decides to come along and strip it like we're going to do, we could have hot food and cool showers by keeping the batteries and water tanks topped off. Most of the crew will probably work during the day, so we'll need to build a place to hide things over across the valley and around the curve some. Paint it the same color as the desert floor or shift some rocks and you've got a place where train engineers will be blind."

"Yeah, okay, I can see that," Stirling said, walking beside him and still touching the skin of the car. "Man, I had no idea that we could get this much material."

"It will take time," Thor said. "And we'll have to be sneaky, because eventually someone will notice pieces missing. Maybe that means we leave the outside shells for a couple of years while we hollow them out, and then let them collapse one day."

"That was my thought," the man said. "Taking the interiors will weaken them, but most are just shells anyway. Maybe we slowly break the cargo cars from the inside and let them fall in like broken lumps. Requires patience sure, like an arson job for the insurance money."

Thor didn't respond to that one. He'd been slightly amazed at the vast number of casual crimes Stirling Chan had apparently committed in his life. As well as the range.

It was almost like he'd wanted to hit every item on some list, just for completeness sake.

Thor wondered if the man had ever robbed a train. Or if he should suggest it at some point so the man wasn't jealous or left short of completing his life's work.

Red climbed the ladder to get into the car, with Thor right behind her, ready to put a hand on her butt for a lift if she needed it. She did not, but she did smile down at him anyway.

Thor blushed. And then went up next. Stirling came up behind him.

Lefty slung the rifle and joined them.

The dim interior of the car hadn't changed in the few days since they'd left. Linemen had checked the insides apparently, but left the cans of food behind, rather than take them.

There were even dirty dishes still in the sink.

"That's far enough," a voice came out of the darkness.

CHAPTER 41

Damn it.

Lefty had just pulled the rifle down off her shoulder so she could rest it out of the way. There was no easy way to move right now.

A shadow detached itself from the front end of the car and moved into the hallway where the bedrooms and bathroom were. A second followed a moment later.

It was dim in here, but Lefty could see the twin bores of a side-by-side shotgun pointed this way. She assumed it looked just like her twin pistols did when she drew them and centered them on someone.

"We were looking for Duff Dubhthaigh, and all you folks just happened to wander along," the first man said.

He was the bigger of the pair. Broader, anyway, as they both looked about as tall as her. The second man had a skinnier build, more like hers, while the nearer man was like Thor.

So not good.

Red had been closest, but she didn't have a gun in her hands. None of them did except Lefty, and that rifle wasn't going to do her much good against four spray patterns of death in these close confines.

"Put the rifle down really slowly, lady," the man said. "And don't do something stupid like go for a pistol or we'll just kill you all and call it good. Probably a reward for you somewhere if we bring back your bodies."

Crap.

"Hands up, the rest of you," the second man spoke.

His voice was higher than the big guy, a tenor instead of a baritone.

Red, Thor, and Stirling did as ordered. Lefty pantomimed with great care as she bent down slowly and set the rifle down on the black, plastic floor with so many dusty footprints on it.

She'd forgotten that they'd leave tracks that anybody coming along might wonder at. Desert dust, rather than what you had on a train.

Someone must have survived, right? Maybe they were coming back?

"Who are you?" she asked as she stepped back and stood up again.

Red was farthest to the left, with Thor and Stirling on her right in a kind of a bowl shape.

Just right for shotguns at short range to wreak mayhem.

"Rail police," the big man replied with a snarl.

Lefty had her hands up like the other three.

"You sure don't look like railroad cops," she offered. "They wear uniforms and have badges on their chest. I should know. Been arrested by them enough times."

Well, never arrested, but certainly seen a few of those uptight bastards to know the look. Not like she was going to tell these punks anything like the truth.

"None of your damned business, lady," he snapped.

"Then why are you here?" she asked, cocking her head a little and smiling. "Who's this Duff fellow you're looking for?"

Maybe dumb and sexy would distract them. She could wiggle her tits and ass, if that got them off their game far enough for her to shoot them.

"Runaway from the north," the guy said. "Got a bounty on his head, dead or alive. Was supposed to be on this train, but they didn't find him or the engineer. Who are you people?"

"Salvagers," Thor spoke up now, causing the big guy to swing that way a little.

Not enough to kill him, but as long as they were talking, they weren't shooting.

Shotguns like that packed a lot of death into a small area, but they had a serious drawback. Those fellows had a total of four shots between them and then had to crack the weapon in half to reload it.

Lefty had twelve bullets she could put through these punks. She could afford to miss a time or two.

"Salvagers?" the man snarled.

"That's right," Thor nodded. "Up from Capazon to inspect the wreck and see how many cars and men we'll need, and what we should just leave here. Didn't hear anything about a crew gone missing. Or bounty hunters."

"Bullshit," the man growled. "There's no train out there to get here from Capazon."

"Didn't come on a train," Thor kept nodding. "See that little wagon we parked by the car? It's got rail wheels underneath so it can run on the rails, but then drop down and cross open ground. We followed the afternoon post train north, but hopped off a ways back to circle around and see where all things had blown to in the storm."

Lefty found herself almost believing the yarn Thor was

spinning. It certainly had that ring of truth that a good grifter developed if she wanted to be successful.

"I think you're full of shit, mister," the man said.

"Hey, don't believe me then," Thor shrugged. "Stirling here can show you."

Lefty had come to respect just how sharp that squishy, little devil was. He transformed himself into a nerdy gearhead in the space of a heartbeat.

"Dude, it's more than just a wagon," Stirling whined. "I've told you about all the stuff I did to soup it up. Nobody else has anything nearly as awesome as I got. I'll race anybody, anytime. Bonus points for half-rail, half-road track. C'mon."

"Wait a damned minute," the leader over there snapped as Stirling turned and started to walk back out the rear, like the most natural thing in the world.

"Hey, you don't get to call me a liar, pal," Stirling called back over a shoulder. "Let's go. I got to show you, since you won't just believe him. Granted, he's a terrible boss most of the time, but he's got the part about the rails right. Then you'll see."

"Damn it, I said stop," the man took a step forward and turned, focused on Stirling's back, like he was measuring the little bastard for one of the barrels of buckshot.

The boss was starting to block the second man, the one who still had his shotgun pointed at her.

Lefty was fast. She saw her opening and gambled that Stirling knew he was about to get shot and would jump clear, because a face full of dirt beat an ass full of lead.

She went for her pistols as she slid a little to the side, hands flashing to the butts like lightning while she used the boss as a shield, hoping it would be enough.

She drew, even as two shots rang out, followed by a third.

Wasn't the roar of the shotguns firing. Those had a much deeper growl, like the dragons in her stories.

These were pops.

Red and Thor had both recognized when the big man concentrated on the thief and forgot about them. The step forward that cut off the second shooter was enough.

Lefty fired anyway, but only because her conscious mind was slower to catch up with her hands. One bullet into each man, but Red and Thor had done the same, with Thor firing two shots just because.

Thankfully, neither of the dying men managed to squeeze their own triggers. Or course, at this range a hunk of soft lead hit you like a rock.

Both men staggered backwards and fell, already dead from the looks of things. The shotguns clattered to the deck and skittered across the floor, one of them bouncing off Thor's rifle before it came to a rest.

"You never told me you were that fast," she accused Thor.

He grinned and shrugged.

"You never asked," he replied.

"Or you, missie," she said to Red.

Red's smile was huge.

"Hey, is it safe?" Stirling called from outside the car.

"It is," Thor called back. "We'll need to grab some towels, and then be pretty quick about dragging the bodies over and throwing them onto your wagon."

"Excuse me?" Stirling's face appeared at the bottom of the door and inspected everything. "What if I don't want these shits bleeding out all over my nice cart."

"They disappeared without a trace," Thor turned and Lefty watched the grim, angry smile on the man's face. "Walked into the desert and were never seen again."

"Oh, shit, yer evil, Thor," Stirling replied. "I like the way you think."

Thor turned to her and grimaced.

She could see a new man emerging. Not the simple lineman he'd been before, or the criminal she was helping shape him into.

A hard killer. Like her, maybe, or who she'd been.

She would need to help remind him to be a good man. Red would help.

"Grab all their gear from whatever cabin they had stashed it in," Thor ordered her. "Anything that you want, including Acheson's books if they're still here. Red, you help her. I'm going for all the food in the pantry and refrigerator."

"Wild animals got in and cleaned the place out?" Stirling asked, maybe a little more nervous than he'd been before.

He'd also seen the change come over Thor. And respected what it meant.

"No," Thor said with a voice like the ancient Gods of Doom. "Terrible, vengeful ghosts of the ancients. This valley is haunted."

Lefty watched his face for a long moment. Hard and deadly.

Then he smiled at her.

"That way, they'll never bother us again," he said in a lighter tone.

Lefty let her breath go as she saw the old Thor still there under that skin.

Everything was going to be all right.

ABOUT THE AUTHOR

Blaze Ward writes science fiction in the Alexandria Station universe (Jessica Keller, The Science Officer, First Centurion Kosnett, etc.) as well as The Corsac Fox and several other science fiction universes. He also writes action-thriller (present day as well as historic). In addition, he's the editor and publisher of Boundary Shock Quarterly Magazine and Thrill Ride Magazine. You can find out more at his website www. blazeward.com, as well as Bluesky, Goodreads, and other places.

Blaze's works are available as ebooks, paper, and audio, and can be found at a variety of online vendors (Kobo, Amazon, and others) as well as the Knotted Road Press website directly. His newsletter comes out monthly and you can also follow his blog and his Patreon on his website. He really enjoys interacting with fans, and looks forward to any and all questions—even ones about his books!

Never miss a release!
If you'd like to be notified of new releases, sign up for my newsletter.

http://www.blazeward.com/newsletter/

Buy More!

Did you know that you can buy directly from the KRP
website?

https://www.knottedroadpress.com/shop/

Connect with Blaze!

Web: www.blazeward.com
Boundary Shock Quarterly (BSQ):
https://www.boundaryshockquarterly.com/

ABOUT KNOTTED ROAD PRESS

Knotted Road Press publishes dynamic fiction set in exotic locations. Our authors cover a wide range of genres including science fiction, fantasy, mystery, literary, and poetry. We also have unique non-fiction voices in genres such as autobiography, business, cookbooks, and how-tos. We offer both DRM-free ebooks and print books for a global readership.

www.KnottedRoadPress.com

www.ingramcontent.com/pod-product-compliance
Lightning Source LLC
Chambersburg PA
CBHW060251100726
47907CB00003B/843